CW00747566

WHERE TWO MOONS MEET

by

Joan F. Latty

Published by

CENTRAL PUBLISHING LIMITED.
West Yorkshire

Paperback ISBN 1903970 24 5

Central Publishing Limited
Royd Street Offices
Milnsbridge
Huddersfield
West Yorkshire
HD3 4QY

www.centralpublishing.co.uk

WHERE TWO MOONS MEET

I used to tell my children stories when they were young. Life is an adventure and you never know what is around the corner.

I live in Gower, Wales – fifteen minutes through a wooded valley to the beach. I love the sea in all its moods. It seems to reflect my own moods and emotions; the highs and the lows.

I have three grown up children living their own lives. I like people and enjoy the company of all ages, though I also like my times of solitude and reflection.

My aim in life is to find meaning in why we are here. I have a personal belief that if we loved enough, miracles could happen, but sadly I fall short of that state.

Joan Latty

Where Two Moons Meet

1

Emma kicked her legs forcibly up in the air willing the swing to go higher and higher. Her body leant backwards driving the swing up and up until she could look over the hedge into the next garden. She could just see the head of her brother's best friend.

"What are you up to?" She paused. "It's no good pretending you're not there. I can see the top of your head. No point in ducking down, I saw you; I know you're there Tony Minster. It's rude not to answer when someone speaks to you. I know you can hear me."

An audible sigh greeted her words. "I'm here all right but I want peace..."

"Why should you have peace when you hassle and pester other people. You're a..." For a moment her verbal ability deserted her. "You're..."

"A what?" he said.

"Where's my bag? You had no right to take it. It's not fair."

"Since when has life been fair?" He made that irritating, one tone whistle which he had just managed to do by sucking air between his front teeth.

"You'll get it when Sir wants to know why I haven't done my maths homework."

"Tell tale."

"I will tell if you don't give it back to me. You'll see Tony Minster. You'll be sorry."

He kept on whistling in that dreary, one note fashion.

Emma drew her breath in with irritation. "You can be so annoying."

"I haven't got whatever you've lost."

"You know that's not true. It was you that took my bag, Tony Minster."

"You'd better ask your brother what he's done with it."

"What do you mean?"

"What I've said. Do go away! I want to get on with my scientific experiment."

"What scientific experiment?"

"For my project."

"That reminds me. What were you doing in the garden last night. I saw you in the dark."

"Anyone would think I had to account to you for my movements."

"So! It's not exactly normal to have a golfing umbrella up in the dark. It wasn't raining you know. There you were, umbrella upside down, standing there as though you were half-witted."

"If you must know I was catching moths. I can't see why it's your business though. You're too nosy by far."

"Go on, pull the other one," said Emma scornfully.

"Well, I' m not asking you to believe me."

That irritating whistle drilled into the air again. "Oh! Stop it."

"Stop what?"

"That whistle." She put her hands up to her ears to dull the sound.

There was silence between them.

"Tell you what. I'll show you one. I've got a beauty in my vivarium - a privet hawk caterpillar."

"That's not a moth."

"Ah! But it will be in time. It'll change into a chrysalis and then into a moth." You could hear the enthusiasm in his voice. "It's a miracle. All I do is feed it privet leaves and then one morning it will have sealed itself into a hard case."

"How boring," said Emma scornfully. "I've got more to do with my time."

"You'd better see who wants you. That's the fourth time someone's been out and called. I 'spect it's your Mum. She's going to be mad with you."

"All right," she said sulkily. "It'll only be to wash the dishes or go and get something from the shop. I thought I'd managed to skip it this time." She dug her hands deeply into her pockets and thrust her lower lip out. "I wish I was a boy. You're lucky."

"What do you mean - lucky!"

"You don't get everybody on to your back checking what you're doing, expecting you to do things around the house."

"That's what you think. Are you a fly on the wall or something?"

"Well David doesn't do a thing."

"Well I'm not David."

"Boys are all the same."

"That's a sweeping generalisation for a start."

It really wasn't fair. Why should girls always be expected to help out and boys always got out of it? There he was, always getting his own way with the television programmes. Sport, sport all the time. Why should he get his own way all the time? Why?

She flung the kitchen door open and it banged back against the units. "Do you want me?"

"I want you to go to the shop for me," said her mother. "It won't take you a minute."

"Why can't you ask David? He's not doing anything."

"I'm asking you."

"It's always me. It's Emma do this, Emma do that. You'd think there was nobody else in the house except me. It's not fair."

"If the shop was two miles down the road I'd feel some sympathy for you. You could have been there and back in the time you've been arguing the toss."

"That's not the principle. You've got it all wrong." She flounced out of the door in a petulant way. "Nobody understands," she said peevishly.

Tony had crossed through the gap in the hedge and stood in the garden. He gave her a smile.

"Sorted it out?"

"I'm fed up, fed up to the back teeth."

"I'd never have guessed," he said sarcastically.

"It's all right for you. If only I was a...."

"A boy," Tony finished triumphantly. "I bet you won't be saying that in a couple of year's time."

She was getting quite pretty he thought. Not bad... "You'd think you were back in Victorian times, not in the era of equal opportunities. Anyone would think you were stuck in a time warp."

"You're just like my Great Gran, always on about how lucky we are. She left school at ten. They wanted her to stay on and teach but her mother said they needed the money so she went into service. She's always on about how fortunate we are in this day and age to have such wonderful opportunities. It's not that I'm on about. It's the difference in the way we're treated. If I want to stay out late, it's where are you going, who you going with, be back at this time and so on. If David says he'll be in late it doesn't seem to make any difference. No one keeps on to him."

"You poor thing." Emma wasn't sure if there was a hint of sarcasm or commiseration in his voice. His face reflected only a deadpan, inscrutable expression. "I should see your Dad about it. It's no good keeping on to me."

"Did I hear you inciting rebellion?" said a familiar voice from the hedge. "I heard what you said."

"People who listen in to conversations in which

4

they're not included never hear anything good about themselves."

"Get out and show yourself, David," said Tony.

"You're always causing trouble, telling tales." said Emma angrily.

"You're always saying that. It's not true. I'm reading the paper before anyone else gets it. There's no need for you to go to the shop. I'm not spying on you. You're getting paranoid."

"That's a long word for a little boy. Give it here." She reached out for the paper and he pulled it away from her and part of the front page tore apart. "You'll be for it."

David waved the paper in the air tantalisingly out of Emma's reach.

"Give it here."

"Give it to her," said Tony and grabbed it from David before he knew what was happening. "Here, Emma, catch."

What would her father say when he saw how badly the front page was torn, thought Emma.

2

Emma was seething with resentment and angry feelings. She felt as though she was going to explode.

David was irritating her to the point of distraction. Whatever he said or did seemed to hit some sore area of discontent, some sensitive nerve. She tried to reason with herself. It was stupid to be so reactive. He wasn't worth it she told herself. She wasn't going to take any notice. He was doing it to annoy her. If she ignored him he would soon get fed up with the game and something else would attract his attention.

But it wasn't like that.

David came in full of unused energy, all ready to spark off a reaction.

"What's pi R squared? I told you she wouldn't know. Silly old Emma doesn't know Pi R squared."

"You're mental."

"Stop calling me names. Do you hear me?"

"What will you do if I don't? Hey!"

He flipped out at her and his nail caught the side of her face. She flew at him fists flailing. He'd gone too far this time.

"I'll get you for that," she said in a higher pitch then she usually spoke in. "You're not going to get away with that."

They were fighting like mad things. Kicking, pinching, pulling hair, thumping, biting. There were no holds barred and they seemed evenly matched.

Their mother came into the room attracted by the noise.

"Whatever are you doing?" she said trying to draw them apart. "You're too old to carry on like this. I'm ashamed of you. You should know better."

Emma tried to get her breath as she glared ferociously at her brother. She felt near to tears but she wasn't going to show them. Defiance fizzled to the surface.

"I'm fed up with this house and this family. I'm getting out of here."

"You'll do no such thing," said her mother. "It's dark outside."

"I don't care. I'm going and I'm never coming back. You'll see."

She rushed to the door and slammed it after her. As she ran down the path she heard her mother's voice, carrying from the front door where she stood.

"I'll get the police on to you, my girl," and voices rose in anger.

She hoped David was getting a telling off. He deserved it.

Emma ran along the lane. It was dark, so dark that she could not see a thing in front of her. It was cold and a bitter wind blustered in her face. She did not notice what was going on around her at first. She was so angry and annoyed about the unfairness of life and what had happened that evening that she was well down the road before natural apprehension asserted itself.

What was that dark, big shape in the shadow of the lane? It could be someone waiting to pounce on her. What was that creaking noise on the other side of the hedge?

Misery was beginning to compound the myriad emotions she felt surging up inside her, dammed up by her fear before.

The headlights of a car brightly illuminated the lane. They dazzled Emma and she put her hand up to her face. The driver dipped them courteously. The man was huddled over the wheel. He looked back and the speed of his car altered, but he must have thought better about stopping. The engine picked up speed and the tail-lights disappeared around the bend.

Emma was frightened. It was so dark. She was alone and had nowhere to go. Her anger had died back and she wished in her heart that she was back at home in the warmth. But she wasn't going to go home yet. She'd show them.

A flicker of unexpressed anger came to the surface and her courage briefly asserted itself. She brushed angry tears away from her eyes. She wasn't going to go home. Nobody cared. David was their favourite. They wouldn't even miss her if she never went home.

They just didn't care.

She was beginning to feel sorry for herself. She recognised the symptoms. She was angry because of her indulgence in self-pity. It was so degrading. Angrily, she remembered the way they had fought. She should have shown her superiority by staying aloof; showing no signs that what he did or said affected her one atom. But she had reacted and now she felt ashamed of her part in the incident.

Another part of her hoped that they were concerned, worried about where she was and worried about her safety. They deserved to feel something. It wasn't really fair the way she'd been treated. She remembered the last words she'd heard.

"I'll get the police, my girl."

Her father would be home by now. She didn't want to worry him. Perhaps her mother had called the police and they were on the look out for her.

'They won't find me' she muttered angrily. 'No way! I'll darken my face like commandos do when they are on a mission into enemy territory, like going behind enemy lines.' She smeared mud on to her face. Nobody would recognise her now. She was putting herself into the fantasy of the occasion. This could be fun after all. 'Not so much noise' she said to herself. 'They'll be on the look out for infiltrators'. There was safety in silence, the silence of imperceptible movement.

A torch would be handy, she thought. Then someone may see the light that would draw attention to where she was.

Darkness came all around her like a blanket. There was safety in darkness. Her eyes had grown accustomed to the night and she could make out isolated shapes of objects that were quite familiar in the day but took on new form and dimension at night.

Over the gate was a lane that led down a rough, stony path to the bay. There were several farms on either side of the narrow lane. Here was their den that they had made in the woods. There was a stony outcrop of rock and at the base was a hollow that ran back into the overhang of rock. David and several of his friends had covered the floor with bracken during the long Summer months and used to meet to discuss what to do that the grown ups did not know about. It was fun to have secret adventures.

She passed the farm and a dilapidated old farm outbuilding in which they'd noticed rusty old machinery. A long time ago they'd investigated the dim, dusty building. There had been hordes of spiders and cobwebs running in all directions to the timbered roof and the concrete, worn floor. They'd walked into them and the webs had broken and stuck to their faces and clothes. She remembered a rat had scuttled across the floor in front of them when the light from the open door fell across the interior of the barn.

It was an old barn with an attached cottage. The farmer had built a new house and this old building had been left derelict. Tonight, she fancied there was a flicker of light from the dim, dark interior. It must be her imagination. Who was likely to be out at this time of night?

The moon was full, high in the sky. The earlier darkness

of the night had given way to a clarity and brightness that was white and revealing. There was the screech of a barn owl and the hunting cry of a stoat. It was eerie and frightening and still more frightening was the movement of light that dimmed and brightened within the old building.

Emma did not wait to see what was about to happen. She ran, ran as fast as she could. Grandpa's words of advice went unheeded. He had been heard to say, "Stick to your ground. Find out what it's all about. You'll only regret it later when you wonder what you've missed. Most things have an explanation."

She was frightened of the unknown. She ran.

She could have sworn that the barn door had opened and a multitude of shapes were capering and gyrating out into the open and towards her. Had they seen her? The thud of her heart echoed loudly in her ears like a muffled bass drum.

She lay face downward in the grass, hardly daring to peep at the strange little people who made their way down the lane hopping and skipping like Dervishes. She had seen a film of these men from India performing their dances. She was frightened that her thudding heart could be heard. It seemed so noisy in her ears and seemed to vibrate in the ground beneath her body.

These strange little men stopped momentarily to lift up something. This they carried in an up-raised position above their heads. The silence of their progression along the grass verge caused her more unease. All their movements were unrelieved by any vocal noise. No audible release of emotion. Just this frenzied dancing. Swinging this still figure above their heads.

Then, in the moonlight, she could pick out a likeness that she could not accept.

It was unbelievable.

It must be an illusion. She had too vivid an imagination.

It was as unreal as a dream. And that unreality was her undoing.

She had to find out the truth. To find out whether that glimpse she had seen of a well known face on the still rigid body was indeed a reality.

Emma got up and followed the rotund, squat, dwarf like creatures. She had no control over the way she was hypnotically drawn by the music and her feet danced to the same beat. Her body felt light, and she felt vague and distant.

The fear for her safety had disappeared like mist carried away by the wind. She followed, discretion to the wind, drawing closer and closer to the people she was following. They stopped every so often and stood unmoving and still. Some of the abandonment had gone out of their dancing.

Emma sensed this change in their outgoingness and it affected her absorption in the dance. The pace had changed. She felt it was time to drop out, but before this thought was carried into effect, she slipped and fell. Down, down she plummeted, spinning like a top, out of control. Bracken and grass brushed against her body. She vainly tried to grab at the bushes and twigs to stop her precipitate fall.

Down and down she spun. The fall seemed endless as though a bottomless pit, an endless void was beneath her.

What had she done?

What would her parents say about this escapade?

She was always being told to take care, as though they expected her to get into trouble. That life was unsafe.

Then she felt as though all air, all solidity had been compressed from her body.

She hit firm ground and knew no more.

3

Emma opened her eyes to a sight that made her start with fright.

The strange little folk that she had been following were grouped around a figure; a figure that had made her register total disbelief when she'd seen it before. She forced herself to look again even though all her emotions were telling her to turn away, to run, to get out.

She looked through her fingers, as though seeking protection from the hands screening her face, at the still figure they were circled around.

It was as she thought. She had not imagined it.

It was her face, her body.

The same face that looked back at her from the mirror when she critically examined her features wondering what hairstyle would suit her best; the same dark eyes, the same auburn hair.

It could not be anyone else.

But this was impossible. Totally impossible.

She could not be here and there at the same time. It defied all known laws.

As though in answer to her thoughts, she noted the birthmark on the right arm. It was conclusive. If she'd asked for any proof then this was it. There could be no mistake.

Emma pinched her body hard. It hurt. She was flesh and bones. She felt the pain as her nails dug deeply into her arm and left a red imprint.

Surely that was proof enough.

What was happening to her?

She pinched herself again and looked from her nail marked arm to the identical figure on the ground.

She felt confused, frightened.

What was going on?

It was odd to look at oneself as though out of body; to be an observer of the physical body, to see oneself as other people saw you.

What could be going on?

She pinched herself again to make sure it was not a dream and that she would wake up in her own room with the old, familiar things around her, the sun slanting in at the low window.

But no, she was still there in the woods looking, like a bystander, at herself. She felt the panic welling up inside her and the familiar need for flight alerting her limbs for action.

Run, get away.

She turned to find her gaze held by a short, squattish figure. She could not break that gaze. It held her, drew her to it like a magnet.

Emma felt herself losing contact with the confusion and the sensation of being out of control. The intensity of her reaction was declining, fading away like a forgotten dream when she was coming awake from a half remembered dream state. The discord was breaking up and giving way to a still peace that surrounded her with its power.

She felt content, happy

She could not resist pinching herself again to make sure this was reality and tried to think herself back in her bedroom with the old, familiar things around her. If this were a dream she'd wake up in her bed. There would be the teddy bear with the pile worn down to the fabric, the curtains with the sprigs of flowers coursing down the print.

It was not to be. The face in front of her did not

disappear. The gentleness and love continued to radiate from the eyes unblinkingly focused on her. The love surrounded her gently and with a rare tenderness.

She did not want to pull away from them. She wanted to sink, to lose herself in their gaze.

Time seemed to stand still. The fear she had felt had given way to stillness and a knowing that all was well. She had no will or desire to break free. She felt warm, unafraid and relaxed. The reassurance that she felt seemed to come from some inner source. All is well. There is nothing to fear. Everything is all right. It was warm and comfortable, hypnotic and peaceful.

"My name is Scan."

There was a break, a silence. No other thoughts came into her mind.

"We have known each other for a long time."

"I'm sorry," said Emma. "I think you've made a mistake. To the best of my knowledge I have not met you before. Of this I am sure."

"One day it will become more clear to you. At present, it is like being in a fog, but I can assure you we are old friends and our relationship has been of a long duration."

Emma felt there was no point in continuing this thought pattern. She had no recollection that they had met before. Yet there was something oddly familiar, some distant, faint memory stirring in the depths of her mind.

"It is written in the transcripts that help will come from one who fits this description –

'Seventh child of a seventh mother.
Look for her, not another.
Red hair, eyes so brown.
She will survive, not drown:
Bob like a cork
Like a queen walk.
Look for the girl with a mark on her shoulder.
She will solve the problems of Thanbodia,

And find the silver bell
Near Tingate Well.
Then all will be revealed.'"

"Well, for a start, I think there's some mistake. There are only four children in my family. I'm not a seventh child. It must be someone else you're looking for."

"I assure you there is no mistake."

There was a brief silence.

"Your mother will be able to give you a clearer picture. Ask her and she may well be able to clarify things."

"And I have not heard of the places you mentioned. I have no idea what you're talking about." Emma felt unsure.

"As I said before, it is written that you have the power to help our country and our people. You may not believe that to be true, but it will become clearer to you in the future. You, as a seventh child, have a more developed psychic ability. Even as we talk that ability is exerting itself. Just think for a moment. We are not conversing verbally. You are a natural telepath. You are unaware that since I have met you we have not spoken one word through the vocal chords but totally through the power of the mind."

He hesitated for a moment as though to allow what had been said to sink in and to be understood.

"You can see beyond the periphery of the normal, the apparent universe, into the beyond, into another dimension. The world we are in is as real as the everyday existence you have with your mother and father. There is no need to be afraid. You understand and see more clearly than most people who live in your world."

Emma felt shocked. What had been said was true.

"You have always been psychic, but as you grew you were made to feel stupid if you showed this ability that you had. The people you mixed with did not understand it.

It became rusty through disuse but even as we have been together this gift has asserted itself without any effort."

Emma felt dazed and a little mystified. What was happening to her?

Scan went on to explain that the race he belonged to had not always communicated in this way. They had been deprived of the power of speech, were mute for a long time because the powers of evil had cast a spell over a whole nation and there had been no way to release that curse. As in most cases of deprivation, other senses develop to compensate for the loss and the telepathic ability had become more highly developed. There was almost no need to converse in any other way but it had restricted their means of talking with people that were not telepathic which was sad. And detracted from what they could do to help other people.

"When you say you are mute does that mean you are unable to talk because you cannot hear what is being said to you."

"That is right. We sense and feel."

The other Thanbodians were watching what was going on, were watching for some softening in her approach, an agreement to help them.

"You will help us?" said Scan in a hopeful, optimistic tone. "Let me tell you our past history and what has been written in the heavens since time began. The outcome is not fixed but there is a basic blueprint that will keep on coming around like a carousel until the pattern has been fulfilled. Our country and its people are moving towards a catastrophe. An opportunity, a climax is drawing close when there is a chance to change what has been happening over the past century. What happens to us will affect not only this part of the world but the extended universe."

He looked at Emma in a shrewd, appraising way. "You feature in this plan. That is why you are here at this time and in this place. There is nothing haphazard about what is happening." He registered the look on her face and added, "There is no need to fear. We will be at your side to support you. You will not be alone."

"That's all very well," said Emma. "I cannot just disappear from where I live. It would cause distress and concern to my parents. Can you imagine the needless unhappiness and pain they would feel not knowing where I was?"

"Your consideration gives me a deep sense of pleasure. You are caring and thoughtful. But it will all be taken care of. There is no need to worry in this way though it is to your credit." He went on. "Do you remember seeing your double? It is an indication of what it will be like. The two worlds co-exist alongside each other. You can be in this world and that one at the same time, parallel dimensions. You are unaware of this but the fact that you do not know of its existence does not mean that it is not there. One part of you is aware, the unconscious part of you."

"It is hard to believe. When and in what way am I in this other world."

"When you go to bed at night your spirit leaves your physical body and enters heaven, or what is called the spirit world, where it helps those who are in need. You belong to a group who help out in this way and you meet up with people whom you have known in a previous life and talk about the problems that are facing you in your everyday existence and get instruction how to deal with them. This goes on all the time."

"So I will not be missed."

"If I get the chance I shall let you look down and see yourself from where you are at this present moment." He hesitated then went on "At night you are unaware of this out of body experience, but your spirit gets nourishment, encouragement to persist and persevere and face bravely what has to be done. It is a type of going home."

Sheer amazement registered on Emma's face as she listened intently to what was being said. The screech of an owl echoed above their heads.

"We Thanbodians…"

They lost contact and Emma realised that something had attracted Scan's attention. Some unaccountable movement had been picked up and there was a struggle to identify what was causing the disturbance. At the same time Emma registered that they were picking up vibratory movements on the surface of their skin, as blind people used their fingertips, which became ultra sensitive when they were reading Braille. She had tried to feel and identify the pinprick markings that were in a book for the visually impaired and had found it well nigh impossible to recognise the number of markings that made up the different letters of the alphabet. And she had heard somewhere that they could also pick up sounds if someone said a syllable or word close to their cheek. They could even recognise colours by a sensation of hot or cold. Red, orange, or yellow were warm colours, varying in intensity, and greens and blues and purples were cold in comparison.

And hadn't Scan and his followers picked up her presence at the dance in which she had taken such an active part.

Then if she believed what they had said, her coming had in some way been foretold. They had been expecting her.

This thought frightened her. It made her feel she had no control over her life. She was like a puppet manipulated by strings. She had no autonomy over her life. Hadn't this been implied in the earlier conversation that they had had? The outcome was indefinite even if she did assist them.

But then whatever happened there was bound to be progress. Change of some sort inevitably happened when people tried, otherwise there would be no point in perseverance or persisting with an objective.

"We must go," said Scan. "There is evil around us. We have been located and followed through the rift in the rock. They are circling around us. It is imperative that we move on." He looked questioningly at her. "Have you come to a decision? We have to be quick. Are we to go on without you or are you with us?"

Emma felt herself swell up with importance. She was needed. Somebody wanted her. It wasn't that she wasn't wanted at home but somehow everything was left unsaid. There were so many spaces and gaps where there should have been words, actions and understanding. She always felt unaccounted for, taken for granted, someone who did not have an identity of her own but conformed and adapted to the wishes and beliefs of others. When did anyone last say that they loved her? Then conversely, when had she said 'I love you' to her mother, father or her brothers and sisters?

"Yes, we do need you," said Scan. "But you must make up your own mind. I do not want to influence you. It must be your decision. If we stay here any longer there will be difficulty in getting back to our own dimension. There is little time left. There is a resistance growing which will be difficult to bridge. We must not delay any longer. Here, take my hand," he murmured quietly.

Emma recognised that he knew that she had come to a decision. There was a pressure building up in the wood that was explosive and dynamic. She knew that this was not the time and place to ask questions.

The group they were in seemed to be compressed into a smaller and tighter space. Around them was a dark, oppressive latency in which squeals, grunts and other obscene noises threateningly thrust towards them. The trees seemed to be alive. Snarling faces writhed and shaped on the gnarled trunks. Faces in agony, in grief, writhing with hate, contorted with vindictiveness etched themselves into the bark.

Emma had seen similar faces on the wooden veneers of furniture. The arms of the trees seemed to be alive, intent to batter, to reach down from their stationary positions and threaten and harm. The undergrowth, the leaves seemed alive with menace. The air seemed thick with threat and the intermittent flash of a million pairs of eyes that were subliminal in effect.

They were there but couldn't be seen.

"We are in acute danger," said Scan. He held Emma's hand firmly and Emma felt safer and more secure at this contact. The menace in the wood grew and grew. The air became heavy and oppressive. It was so hot that it was difficult to breathe.

Brambles tore at Emma's legs and scratched her face. Nettles stung the open, exposed parts of her body and bit through her lighter clothing. A bat fluttered in her face. Emma frantically brushed the loathsome creature away. The smell of must lingered on her fingers at the point where she had touched the soft body.

More came to the attack, swooping up and down, touching her face with their wings and tangling in her loose, long hair.

The oppressiveness and the noise grew so intense that sound seemed to dominate her sensory functions. There was nothing else in existence, only this barrage of noise. It was so dominant and intrusive that it caused her actual physical pain. Her head felt as though it was going to explode and she vainly put her hand up to her head as though to ensure it was in one piece and she wanted to release this pain by screaming and screaming until it all stopped.

Scan, recognising the trouble she was in, plugged her ears with something soft and malleable that had the effect of lessening the severity of the noise. She was overwhelmed with gratitude. She could put up with the ringing in her ears now that the overwhelming ear splitting noise had eased. That was nothing in comparison. It was merely uncomfortable. Her confusion and panic lessened and her heartbeat stopped pounding in her chest like a big bass drum.

They struggled on for what seemed an endless space of time. The distance they covered was microscopic. There were so many pressures dragging them back that their bodies were unable to progress forward.

Emma felt frightened. The pressure on her body felt destructive. Could it tear her apart, pull her to pieces? Could she possibly no longer be?

On and on they pressed as though pushing against an immovable force barrier. There were pricks, punches, pinches, tearing, scratching, pulling. Her whole body surface felt as though it was disintegrating and would be unrecognisable. Would she look the same after this terrible ordeal? Would she be identifiable?

She could no longer lift her limbs or move forward. It was as though she was stuck in some time warp from which she would never exit.

Then, as she thought all was over, there was a lessening in the pressure, an ease in the way she being thrust up against an impenetrable obstacle. She could move her distorted face, had control over her wayward limbs which had been disordered and without function.

The ground was firm beneath her feet.

And she heard Scan's melodic voice reassuring her and a soft, gentle peaceful balm surrounded her and soothing her tired, exhausted body.

"We are nearly through," said Scan. "The healing, helpful rays are reaching out to us giving us strength and assisting our passage."

She was swirled, upheld in a soothing mist that embraced and penetrated the cells of her body. She felt lighter as though she had no substance and all the physical pain and mental distress had disappeared. Her fatigue had gone.

Beneath her feet were the bracken fronds that they had cut to cover the floor of the cave where the gang used to meet. It had been their den. The fronds were brown and dry now. The cave led into the limestone rocks that towered high above the valley in a stony outcrop that led down to the sea.

There were many swallow holes that were wide and high enough for a person to stand upright, deep underground. They had been expressly told on no account to go into these openings and there were stories of a Jack Russell dog that had disappeared and had never been seen again.

"This is where we used to meet, to discuss, make plans for the holidays," said Emma with obvious surprise at recognising where she was.

"We have watched and waited until the time was right." With these words, Scan and his followers disappeared.

Emma felt lonely and frightened. Panic welled up inside her. She wanted to run, to get away but inside her was the still, small voice.

"All will be well. We will take care of you."

Emma felt herself struggling against the sleep that threatened to overwhelm her and her eyelids refused to stay open, even though she consciously willed her eyes to look at her surroundings and not give in to this tiredness. She had to... and the words petered out and her awareness had gone.

She slept on the piled up bracken on the floor.

4

Emma awoke with a start. It took some time to realise where she was and her thought processes to remember what had happened the previous night. She looked through slitted eyes at the scene. She expected to see the moss covered stone and the bracken covered floor. This was a different cave. It was dry. There was more light. Light that cast a prismatic coloured movement with an undertone of flickering green, which was like a living thing.

Over her was a swatch of material. It was gossamer thin but luxuriously soft to the touch. She pulled it up to her face comfortingly and ran her fingers along the fine edges. As a child she had done the same thing with the sheet on her bed. In her insecurity she had automatically reverted to a long outworn habit.

It seemed a lifetime away.

Misery and despair welled up inside again. She felt lonely and homesick. A dull ache made her long for home and the people she had left behind. She tried to restrain the misery, but the tears and sobs wracked her body with their intensity.

This was how Scan found her.

"Why so sad little one?"

"I want to go home. I do not like it here."

A look of open disappointment registered on Scan's face.

"That is your prerogative. Your help has to be freely given without any coercion or force otherwise your presence would be worthless. Here come to me." His outstretched arms drew her like a magnet. "Let me show you our world."

The instant impression Emma had was one of greenness, vast tracts of green meadow. Not grass, she found when she bent down and pulled a handful, but a herb which smelt of the orangey camomile and the wild thyme when they were bruised. They were fragrant and sweet.

There was water everywhere. A fine spray from waterfalls that cascaded down the slopes with dolphin-like movements into still pools, crystal clear, where the shimmer of scales mirrored the movement of many fishes darting among the weeds. Rainbows arched their Gothic way across the sky. The area of their base was not as wide as the rainbows that Emma was used to. It was a multi-coloured world and her heart soared at the visual beauty of what lay before her.

"You like our world?" said Scan.

Emma had no words to describe the beauty of what was in front of her. The scenery seemed more compressed than that which she had previously experienced - rugged cliffs, towering mountains, gently inclined fields that were matchbox sized, like a gauge N railway.

In her seven league boots she could cross mountains and valleys and be part of it in a short time. There was no distance. It was all there in front of her, but a giant like immobility made her fear the damage her ungainly feet could cause.

Scan laughed a pure ripple of sound.

"You like our country? Yes! It is peaceful and tranquil now, but for nine months of the year the beauty of this valley is obscured with snow and ice. Blizzards tear at the greenery and landslides alter the contours of the valley. It was not always so, but much evil and despair has occurred within our land. Xylo has us within his power. To avoid destruction we have to live a nomadic existence, to be continually on the move. We have lost our roots." He looked up at the dark, lowering sky. "The weather is about to change. There will soon be snowdrifts driving in from the northeast. The well known landmarks will disappear and be obscured by the thick snow."

He looked up again at the thickening clouds that were getting darker and more oppressive and hung threateningly low over the valley.

"We must move on. This change in the weather brings its own terrors. The snow watchers are aware of our vulnerability and the way our movements are slowed down. They will be on the look out for stragglers and strangers. They send out parties of trained killers who have no pity on those they catch. They capture and maim and kill indiscriminately. They will by now have recognised there is something different about the landscape and will have been sent out to check what is happening."

He abruptly blanked out from her. A worried, surprised look appeared on his face. He turned brusquely to the person who had appeared alongside them.

"Who is this?"

"David! It can't be you!" said Emma. "David!" and she flung her arms around him warmly. "How did you get here?"

David was about to answer when a man came forward hastily.

"Let me explain." He indicated David with a friendly look of appraisal. "He was in the cave in the wood and I felt there was a chance that the two worlds were still bridged together across the two dimensions and we were fearful that he would find his way into our world and get lost."

"You should have known better than that," said Scan. "There was no danger of that happening. Now he will have to remain and be one with us."

Emma's face beamed with delight. "I'm so pleased to see you. It seems such a long time since we had that quarrel and I walked out."

"I don't understand what you are talking about. I saw you at breakfast. Grouchy you were too."

A look of disbelief registered on Emma's face but she did not say anything. Her time scale was upside down and there were so many areas of confusion. It did not make sense.

"Never mind," she said. "You are here now and I'm so glad to see you."

She did not catch the incredulous disbelief that registered on David's face as he listened to what she had said. "Anyway what were you doing in the cave at this time in the morning?" said Emma. "It's usual for you to lie in until the sun is well up."

"We'd planned to get together to decide whether you could join the gang. The hols coming up it didn't seem fair to leave you out of things."

"Very gracious of you," she said sarcastically. "You'd think I was going to be the only girl in the gang."

"Well! You're my sister."

"So what! What difference does that make? If you had any sense of family you'd stand up for me not always put me down."

"But you've always got so much to say for yourself and," he added, "you side with the others against me, so you can talk."

"Rubbish!" said Emma heatedly.

"There's no time for arguments," said Scan. "I see dots in the sky. They are Xylo's scouts on the look out for stragglers. They mercilessly scour the countryside and capture anybody they see. They select some as slaves; the ones they recognise as being more susceptible to suggestion, and more easily programmed to do as they say. The others they kill." He hesitated for a moment. "They are never the same, once they are taken prisoner. They become changelings and are sent out to spy and report back on what they have found. They come among us and pretend to be our own." He looked at David and Emma. "There is one thing we have to do before we go further. To make you one of us."

Scan registered the doubt on Emma's face.

"It will be all right. There will be no danger to you. It will only be a temporary measure."

Emma looked at the countryside that she had been longing to explore.

Scan said, "I see you want to stay big, to be a giant in Lilliput land. Perhaps one day, when it is less dangerous. I fear for your safety. You stand out like trees on the skyline when winter has left the branches gaunt and bare. Their starkness attracts the eye. Your presence will be unmistakable. Those dots you see are Xylo's spies sent to investigate. To find out what those changes mean. Come we must go. Make haste to the shelter of the woods. Take this liquid. It will make you our size. Then there will be less danger to us all."

It was a green, opalescent liquid with clear bubbles, not like the fizz in lemonade, but like the globules that form when oil is added to water or orange juice. They moved around, these bubbles with an activity of their own, changing shape, dividing into two, decreasing into one and then splitting again into numerous numbers. The liquid had a hypnotic attraction of its own.

"Do they want us to take it?" said David with a questioning look. "Well, I'm not sure. Oh, in for a penny, in for a pound!" and he swallowed the liquid. Emma followed suit. There was no point in being squeamish.

Nothing happened. Everything was just the same. Then Emma realised that the grass was tall above her head and that the camomile and thyme were waist high. An ant ran up a tall grass and balanced precariously above her head. She was pint sized in a green jungle.

"I can't help thinking it would have been more time efficient to have put you in our pockets. We could have made it to the woods much more quickly."

"That may be true but it would have been more dangerous. It would have drawn attention to our whereabouts. That would have put us in a difficult position."

"Emma," said David. "Why don't they speak?"

Emma could not conceal the smile that was giving away how she felt. David was not telepathic. He could not follow what was being said. Her conversation with Scan had passed unnoticed. This was one field where she could excel.

"We have a problem," she said to Scan.

"Yes, I have already noticed that there is a difficulty. We can sometimes project a thought into someone's mind but they cannot project anything back. There is such a conglomerate of disassociated thoughts, that the idea, the thought goes unnoticed and joins the general stream of chaotic thought patterns that bubble up endlessly. You are a telepath natural. Others have a latent skill that can develop with encouragement. It is there in all humans but logic and analytic skills have rendered it an occult, hidden ability. It is more highly developed in you and even in the time we have known you it has become easier to communicate. You will need to act as a go-between and keep David in the picture."

David was becoming more and more irritated. "Anybody would think I had some communicable disease," he whined. "Nobody takes any notice of what I say. Anybody would think I was invisible. Perhaps that funny tasting liquid..." The sentence remained unfinished and a look of fear registered on his face.

'Ah ha!' thought Emma. Perhaps this was a chance to break even, to redress the balance. Now, what if she pretended that everything that David said was not said had gone unheard?

"Em! Can't you hear what I am saying?" He was becoming red in the face with anger and fear. His fists were clenched in tight balls and the level of his voice had changed. "You're ignorant, plain ignorant. Might as well talk to a wall."

Emma smiled enigmatically to herself. "Where's David? He seems to have disappeared."

"There's nothing to smile or laugh about," yelled David. "I've had enough of this nonsense I can tell you. You've not merely got smaller, your brain has atrophied, got smaller and you've lost the ability to use it. What's the point? Why did I have to have a sister? Girls are one law unto themselves." He took a deep breath. "You make me sick," he yelled in exasperation. "Do you hear me?" and his voice rose to a crescendo. "You make me sick. Do you hear me, sick!"

"I wonder where he's gone?" said Emma quizzically. "David, David where are you?"

"That's enough," said Scan. "Your brother is getting angry and frightened. You've had your fun Emma." He turned and smiled at David. It made Emma think of a game of pork sausage that they used to play. It went something like this.

"Where are you going?"

"Pork sausage."

"Is Mum in?"

"Pork sausage."

"I hear you have a girl friend."

"Pork sausage."

And so it went on. Emma knew how exasperating this could be.

Another irritating version: -

"Are you going down the shop?" David asked.

"Are you going down the shop?" repeated Emma.

"I asked you a question."

"I asked you a question," repeated Emma.

"Stop it."

"Stop it," repeated Emma.

"You're a pest," said David heatedly. "You get your kicks from annoying people."

"You're a pest..." repeated Emma. And so on.

The only thing to do was to turn and go, to ignore the person and not take part in any exchange. This is what David had done.

Emma laughed in a mischievous way. "I was only having you on." She wondered whether she ought to tell him the situation. It would be good to have this one over him but a reproving look from Scan made her mind up. "Scan and his people are telepathic. He noticed that you were getting distressed and he told me to explain the situation. I couldn't resist having you on. It was too good an opportunity to miss." She started to shriek with laughter. "You did look funny. If you'd been in my shoes you'd have done the same thing. There's no need to be so cross," she said and laughed again in an irrepressible way.

"You pig," said David.

Scan moved towards them with open, outstretched arms which he changed to hands together in the prayer position in front of his chest. There was a Buddhist element about the approach.

"Does David understand why we are unable to communicate with him," Scan asked Emma.

"Yes," said Emma, grinning in her characteristic, mischievous way. "For the first time, it seems I have all the aces in the pack."

"We have delayed too long," said Scan. "It will cost us dearly. The dots on the horizon are getting larger and larger. Our only hope is to make for the woods without delay. There we will have some cover. Quick. Follow me."

The stones on the mountainside ran before them as they scrambled down the steep sided valley. The noise echoed from the opposite wall of the valley and more stones cascaded down disturbed by the movement of their stumbling feet.

"Tread carefully," said Scan. "Once we are over this ridge we'll be in a safer position. The trees fringe the edge of the ravine. The creatures are getting closer and closer. I can see clearly the outline of their wings black against the whiteness of the sky."

Their dark forbidding shapes loomed nearer and nearer. Emma could hear the noisy screeches they made and a dark shadow was cutting out the light in the sky. Emma looked around. She could make out the row of joined dorsal spikes on the upper part of the body and the long, taloned feet dangling below their ugly under parts. Their bodies were coarse and scaly. Their prehistoric, pterodactyl appearance terrified her. It was like something from a bygone era.

Her paralytic fear froze her movements nearly to a standstill. She was irresistibly drawn to have another look, and that was her downfall. She stumbled and fell. Her feet spun from underneath her.

The last words she heard as she plummeted to the ground were "They are upon us."

Emma lay where she had fallen, not daring to move, immobile, frozen face to the ground. She heard the rush of wings through the sky. The peculiar magnified bat-like sound rending the air with its piercing quality.

She forgot about the others, aware only of the danger she was in and the fear that she was going to die. She was alone with this horrific experience. No one could share this moment of utter terror.

She could smell the ammoniacal, acrid stench that hung in the air. It stung her nostrils and filled her with revulsion and disgust. She felt sick and her body heaved mechanically. Tears ran down her cheeks involuntarily.

She wanted to run, to get away, but she could not move.

The brush of something scratchy fell across her body. This was it, she thought, but nothing happened. She knew she had to keep still and not betray her position. There was something on top of her. She felt the increased weight and the sharpness and scratchiness hurt her bare skin.

She wanted to move, to throw off what was holding her down, but above her was the sound of wing movement and the agonising human screech of terror. She kept as still as possible. Her limbs were aching and painful from the forced rigidity and she began to tremble uncontrollably. She wanted so much to move but she knew that she was in great danger.

It was essential that she kept still. The screeches and screams of terror made her shiver as though her blood had been turned to ice and her hair stood up on the back of her neck.

Then she realised that the sounds and the noise had subsided. She listened more intently. There was a wind coming up and as Emma moved she saw the flurry of snow crystals on her arm. There was a low moan from scarcely a foot away, and the pitiful cry of pain repeated time and time again. She asked herself was it safe to move? The screeching and movement of wings had gone.

She moved fractionally to better see what was going on around her. There seemed to be a tangle of bramble over her that scratched at the exposed, vulnerable parts of her body when she moved. Her face felt sore and when she brushed her hand upward to remove the hair from her eyes. It was red with blood.

There was a murmur of movement like wind in the long grass or music in the reed beds and Emma knew instinctively and with a heart filling humility that in her hour of need she had been helped. The bramble canes had moved from over her to their original position.

She could move.

Cautiously Emma looked around her. One of Scan's

followers lay on the ground, his body partially covered by the falling snow. She edged towards him. His face was scratched and covered with blood. His eye lay exposed on his face and the eye socket was a gory mess. Extensive scratch marks ran in parallel fashion the length of his face.

She turned away in horror. Her thoughts were invaded by a pleading request. "Do not turn away. Please help me, I beg you."

She wanted to run away, to turn her back on the scene before her, but she could not do this. Something nagged inside her urging her to face the situation.

The injured man lay on the ground. The stench, the grass running with gore and blood, the butchery, the destruction and pointless waste of life around her were more than she could bear. And the whiteness of the snow highlighted dramatically the contrasting colour of blood.

She courageously battled with her fear and knelt down on the snow-covered ground. The flakes were falling more densely, so much so that her vision was blurred by the flurry of movement.

Emma tried to stifle, to swallow down the panic inside her. "I will do what I can but I do not know where we are, or where to turn to get help."

She suddenly realised with fear that everyone she was close to had disappeared. She was alone with an injured man, in a strange land. The weather was changing for the worse and the existing landscape was losing shape and structure. There were no visible pathways.

"It is snowing," she said, "and I cannot make out which direction to take."

"The night of darkness is upon us," said the man. "We must find shelter otherwise we will die. The way I am, death may be kinder but you must find safety and warmth. You have a job to do and it is my responsibility to see you reach the others without unnecessary delay."

"You think they may be still alive?" said Emma, a

note of hope in her voice.

The man staggered to his feet. The pain and cold reflected on the undamaged side of his face. Emma tried to look at him but the sight of his trammelled, scored face made her look away. The sight was too horrible. Blood, a dull, dark, red fell on the white snow.

He stood swaying into an upright position.

"In that direction where the wood angles up against the sky. That is the way to go. You will have to support me. I am weak but do not fear. We will get there."

Emma noticed the clenching of his jaw. She wished she had the same faith that gave him the determination to forge ahead with purpose despite his severe injuries.

There was no pathway.

Kyoto, for that was his name stopped periodically, head in the air as though taking his bearings. Emma could see nothing, only snowflakes that drifted to a point in front of her eyes and hypnotically they mesmerised her senses.

They trudged on falling into snowdrifts and wearily dragging themselves out again. There seemed to be no end to the white wilderness in front of them. A bird with the markings of a magpie flew screeching above their heads.

Kyoto looked in the direction from which the bird had flown. There was not a movement. They were nearer the woods now.

Emma felt her strength flagging and had to push herself to continue.

"Stop," she said. "Stop. I cannot go any further. I must rest."

Kyoto looked sternly at her.

"There is no possibility of rest. Sleep in this snow and you will never wake up. Your limbs will grow colder and colder. Your sleep will become deeper and deeper and gradually your breath will fade away. Our only chance of staying alive is to keep moving. Take courage. The shelter of the trees is ahead of us. I sense that Scan is ahead of us too."

Emma was overcome with weariness. All she wanted to do was sink to the ground, to rest, to sleep, to give way to this intolerable tiredness. She did not care what happened. As long as she could put her head down and rest.

Kyoto was plodding on ahead. She had to stay with him. To be alone was a thought too intolerable to bear. He was a companion and where he went she would go also.

Then the intolerable happened. Kyoto fell in an impassive, unmoving heap on the dense, packed snow. She beseeched him not to die, to get up, but he lay unmoving and still.

"Please, please get up. You must get up. You must not give up now. Please," she begged on her knees beside his still form.

He lay silent and misshapen on the white surface. She sat back on her heels. Tears coursed down her face and dropped on to her hands. One fell on Kyoto's face and he stirred.

She saw the movement and vigorously shook him, forgetful of his injuries; only aware of the danger they were in.

"Wake up! Wake up!" but he was impassive, seemingly unaware of the fear that was influencing her behaviour.

The snow lay along the branches of the trees. She had always wanted snow in winter, to make snowmen, snowballs, to slip and skate, to sleigh and toboggan. She had tried one year when there'd only been a smattering of snow to toboggan down the slope in the farmer's field on an old tin tray which had been manufactured by a special process, and Mum and Dad had been cross with her for damaging it. She'd pleaded with Dad to make a sledge but before he'd finished it the snow had gone. The sledge had been in the garage for years waiting for snow to fall.

Snow, she thought. Emma at that moment wanted to

see Mum and Dad more than anything else. A tear coursed down her cheek. She wanted to go home. Then an idea came into her mind. Why couldn't she make a sledge? There was plenty of wood and trailing vines, though the snow was filigreeing them into unusual shapes. If only she had more strength, she thought, as she reached above her head and the snow cascaded in a flurry of powder down upon her, disturbed by the movement. The powder turned to wetness and her tongue touched at it tentatively.

She suddenly realised she was thirsty. She reached at the overhead vines once more. Her fingers were getting numb and cold. She forced them to tie the vines around the wood.

If only she was stronger. Her energy seemed to be draining away. She clenched her jaw with sheer determination and willed her unruly, undisciplined fingers to do as they were told. All she wanted to do was give up but something inside her willed her to keep going.

"You are doing well. Do not give in. I know you want to rest but lie down in the snow and you will die."

"I am so tired," she said. "So tired. Even in this cold I would give anything to just curl up and close my eyes."

"That would be fatal. There is a job in front of you. If you give up it will affect the outcome not only of what you have to do but many others who walk alongside you will be affected by that decision. There are many people prepared to assist you. Even now you do not walk alone. You may not believe this but it is a fact. Know you are loved. Walk upright and straight with this knowledge in your heart and be brave and strong. You are not alone."

As Emma listened her fingers seemed to work with increased agility. It was with surprise that she looked at the sledge she had somehow constructed. Not a work of art but it was functional. It served its purpose. She began to feel that after all she at least possessed perseverance and determination, if nothing else, and her spirits rose at the thought. A silvery laugh bubbled up inside her.

Kyoto lay blue and cold on the snow. The snow crystals were drifting over his still form. How much more could he take?

Everything was still and noiseless. No sign of life, not even a bird flew from the snow-impacted hedges. She was the only living, breathing thing that seemed to exist. She was alone in this icy wilderness with only Kyoto as a companion. Even though he was unconscious his presence eased the isolation she felt.

Emma dragged his still, inert body on to the roughly made sledge. The weight and energy she exerted made her breathless and she stopped until her ragged breath returned to normal.

Her breath was white on the cold air. Her arms and hands were blistered and torn and to do anything with them was painful, and she flinched as the pain seared through her when she tried to use them to secure Kyoto safely to the sledge and prevent him from falling off when she started to move.

Her legs ached and they felt stiff and clumsy. Every footstep was an intolerable effort. Every so often her legs gave way beneath her and she fell into the deepening snow. Each time it happened it seemed more difficult to get up, and more of a struggle to get moving again. She had no sense of direction. Just a dogged, driving force which would not let her give up. The knowledge that she had to keep going. She had to get through.

5

Meanwhile Scan and David had managed to keep together. They had reached the safety of the wooded area. It was each man for himself before the fearful onslaught of Xylo's bat like creatures.

There was terror in their hearts as they hurtled down the slope followed by the screeching cries and the heavy beat of wings in pursuit, so near that they could smell the acrid stench of their breath, hot on their necks.

They waited under the cool forest trees, waited and hoped that others would follow, that others had survived. Indeed, some caught up with them and were greeted with warmth and affection but many were left unaccounted for. A search party was sent out to check for any survivors and they came back with grim tales of death and destruction. So it was, with heavy hearts that they gave up looking at the empty tracts of snow and decided to move on. They felt that adequate time had been given for any surviving stragglers to catch up.

There was no sign of movement, no sign that there was anything living, the way that they had come.

They assessed their losses - Kyoto, Emma, Rondo and several others. Rondo was a loss to them because he was level-headed and capable. He was always foremost with ideas and action. They realised at this time that mourning was wasteful, so, inwardly sorrowing at the narrowing of their numbers, they forged ahead out of the snow and into the valley where Xylo did not have the same influence and power.

The ragwort and the red campion swung in the breeze and the air was sweet, balmy and soft. They rested on the springy turf and looked in the direction they had come with a vain hope that they would see a few more of their people coming towards them. The horizon was empty; no figures were silhouetted against the white sky.

And then they saw a movement, a movement that they could not distinguish. A dark cloud was coming closer and closer to them. It was so dark that it blocked out the rays of the sun and it carried with it an oppressive, foreboding sensation. They registered that the safest thing to do would be to get out of range, to run, but whatever it was, it moved too swiftly.

They were upon them.

Millions of flies slashed into their eyes, their mouths, were drawn into their nostrils as they breathed, crawled into their ears. There were millions of these creatures, like dense armies of flying ants or locusts. As they brushed them away, thousands more were taking their place.

In the midst of his misery, David felt there was some sense of reassurance getting through to him. He somehow knew that the insects meant him no harm. They were passing through. The sudden change in the weather had caught them unawares and they were making their way to the warmer regions.

They were not attacking. The cold wintry weather had surprised them as much as Scan and his followers.

Half drowsy and dropping by the thousands on the journey they littered the surface of the area with what looked like a pathway trailing behind them as far as the eye could see. They flew instinctively towards the warmer climate and as they flew, they swarmed and crawled over everything in their path. The sky was darkened by their movement.

The initial panic David had felt subsided when the realisation dawned that the discomfort would soon be over.

David shook his head vigorously to keep the insects from settling on his face and pretended that each hair was whip-sized, like a cow's tail flicking backward and forward disturbing the flies and preventing them from settling. He knew now why the black and white cows in the field behind his house flicked so furiously with their tails. How uncomfortable it must be, even though their hides were thicker and less sensitive. At last the numbers began to decrease, only a few stragglers buzzed past.

Then it was all over and they sprawled on the green grass, easing the tension from their tired bodies. They didn't realise how tired they were, and how much their exhausted bodies craved rest.

They awoke much later to the eerie screech of an owl. The trees rustled in the wind and the grass rippled like a moving sea. Their eyes grew accustomed to the darkness and they could make out the shapes and shadows of trees, shrub and undergrowth, and the purple of mountains in the distance.

An unexpected movement made them freeze into immobility, too frightened to move, the beat of their own hearts loud in their ears until they realised that there was no immediate danger in the vicinity.

They were alone under the still, cold, star-peppered sky. They relaxed and rested peacefully, until the cold light of dawn settled over the dew-wet countryside.

6

Scan and his followers looked searchingly back along the way that they had come, vainly hoping that there would be some sign of Emma against the skyline. The plain was deserted and uninhabited.

Scan recognised that his priorities lay ahead. They could not wait indefinitely. There was safety in movement. They could not so easily be pinned down by the innumerable lookouts that worked for Xylo.

"We have to move on," said Scan to his followers. "I am convinced that Emma is alive."

The others were sceptical about this and looked at each other in a knowing way and nodded their heads pessimistically. There was no point in dispelling his hope, but they knew better. Hadn't they seen the devastation that was always left after one of these attacks, and to be kept as a prisoner that was even worse, to endure the humiliation of captivity and all it entailed.

David wept unashamedly. Tears ran down his cheeks and channelled their way to the corner of his mouth. Up until now he had always been at odds with Emma, thought she was a nuisance, got in the way, took all the attention, but now he longed to see her pert face at his elbow and hear her voice. She had gone from his life and under the circumstances what was left was a painful void. He would not see her again. He somehow felt personally responsible for not taking more care of her.

There was no one to quarrel with, to try out his newly found masculinity. He had to admit that Emma was changing, becoming more feminine, or perhaps he noticed these things more. That could be the reason. On the other hand, he had noticed that she stood for what seemed like hours in front of the mirror looking at this and that side of her face critically and trying her hair in different ways and never seeming satisfied with the result. He'd noticed that her eyes would follow the boys as they passed in a coquettish type of way. She took ages deciding what to wear when she was going out.

It was his friend whom had drawn attention to this by saying in an offhand manner that Emma was becoming quite attractive.

"What her?" he'd answered. "You must be off your head," but he'd looked at her in critical appraisal to confirm or disapprove the suggestion. She wasn't bad, he'd thought, not bad, not bad at all.

He missed her. He knew now that his teasing and bantering had sometimes gone too far, but on the whole she'd put up with it in a good-natured way. Sometimes Emma erupted with volcanic rage that ended in blows and tears then he knew he'd pushed his luck too far.

David wanted to remain behind and see if she turned up but he knew they could not afford to hang and loiter around indefinitely. If it hadn't been for Emma he wouldn't be here in the first place. She always managed to cause trouble. It seemed to follow her around. It was her fault really, though she'd be the last to admit it. Perhaps there was an element of being in the wrong place at the wrong time. No one had coerced him to be there. It just happened.

He glanced surreptitiously behind him in the vain hope that Emma had materialised out of thin air. Why couldn't she use those psychic powers she was said to have, make them work for her and perhaps, better still, get them to protect her at a time like this?

"Seventh child of a seventh mother.

Red hair, eyes so brown.

She will survive not drown,
Bob like a cork.
Like a queen walk.
Look for the girl with a mark on her shoulder.
She will solve the problem of Thanbodia,
And find the silver bell,
Near Tingate Well."

The rhyme had foretold that good would overcome evil. The threat to the Thanbodian race would be overcome. Emma had a major part to play in what was about to happen. Was there a chance that they would meet up again? On consideration, David thought not.

He remembered the carnage, the horrific scene which had met their eyes when they had gone back to look for survivors after the attack by the creatures of Xylo. They had checked the mutilated bodies, which were hardly recognisable, to see if Emma had been one of the victims left as dead.

She had not been among them and their relief was spliced with emotional distress at the thought that she could have been taken prisoner. They had sadly left the area where the attack had happened knowing that they had to move on. They had covered a major amount of ground but despite the distance, they were still in danger. There was always the risk of their betrayal. They had continually to be on the alert for attackers.

They were the pursued, lurking in the underbrush, under the trees in the wood, making for the shelter of the coppice. Their lives were the existence of a fugitive, an escaped prisoner on the run suffering from that apprehensive fear that every hand on the shoulder, every enquiry had recognition of who they were, and that they would be taken prisoner again.

This type of existence, living on fear, was exhausting and debilitating. David had never drawn much credit for his standard of cross-country. His feet showed signs of rubbing and blistering. Each movement, each step was excruciatingly painful. He limped in a vain effort to take the pressure off the painful areas without much effect.

Tall hemlock with its umbrella, inverted, wheel-like heads, flat, sweet scented meadowsweet and tall grasses stretched before them in endless sweet smelling plains. The wind moved over the grasses in a wave movement, flattening the grasses that moved back into position once it had passed, dipping and cresting. Then, one morning, David heard the unmistakable sound of running water.

The tinkle of a waterfall was as clear as crystal on the bright early morning air. He imagined the stream plummeting, cascading down into a pool where the turbulence gave way to a deep, unmoving stillness and he longed to throw off his clothes and dive into the deep, cool waters and feel the caress of the chevron as his body sank into the depths.

The picture was a torment.

Scan had told them not to wander off on their own but to stay together. The sound of water and the pictorial images which kept flashing into his mind were making David divided within himself. He longed for water with an external and internal hankering. The mucous surfaces of his mouth seemed to stick together and his skin felt hot, dry and burnt.

The Thanbodians had a dislike, a dread of water. They avoided it as David had a fear of fire. They had watched David bathing in a stream with open horror and twitterings of fear. How could they understand his preoccupation, which almost seemed an obsession? They had thrown up their hands and shook their heads in a desperate attempt to express their horror and fear.

David had laughed. Soap and water was a totally different thing, behind your ears, under your chin. He had a horror of this type of confrontation. Perhaps that could be the reason. Perhaps too much attention had been drawn to keeping clean when they had been young and this had created this distaste for things wet.

The sound of running water was too much for him to ignore. He gave way to temptation and crept on tiptoe, the sound growing louder with each footstep. There was still no sign of the stream, just endless tracts of grassland. No landmarks stood out on the landscape to indicate the direction he had followed, and after some distance he started to feel uneasy. There was no water in sight.

He turned to go back but the grasses that had bent beneath his footsteps had sprung back and there was no sign of the way he had come. He felt tired and weary and he lay down on the sweet scented grass and the warmth relaxed his tired body and he fell soundly asleep.

Raindrops pattering on his face awoke David from a sleep where he was pursued by evil beings. He was hiding and they were looking for him, covering every square inch of ground with a thoroughness which made his hair rise in hackles on the back of his neck. They were scarce a foot away from him when suddenly he awoke to an awesome sight. In front of him was a glittering figure, all silver, covered in filigreed tinfoil, patterned with intricate designs. She stood over him, the glow around her so intense that David found difficulty in looking at her, as though he was looking at the sun.

"Do not fear. I come to do you no harm." She soothed his forehead with cool, gentle fingers, brushing the hair with soft movements back from his brow. "You are tired." She ran her fingers through his hair again. "I will bring you peace and strength. Just lie back."

David felt himself responding to the calm, gentle, hypnotic movements. There was a fluidity about her that curved around him and made him feel enclosed and comfortable. Something made him struggle against the overwhelming need for sleep, sleep that would not let him keep his eyelids open. He fought the intensity of his need and tried to register what was going on around him but his vision blurred and his eyelids closed. The last thought he had in his mind was that he must get back to Scan and his followers. He should not have gone off on his own. It had been a foolish thing to do. He had been warned. He struggled against the sleep but it was like a vice holding him firmly in its teeth.

"There is no point in struggling," said the same level, throaty, hypnotic voice. "You are mine, down in the weeds at the bottom of the pond. Your hair floats behind you. You are dead, one of the other world, a Will o' the Wisp."

"I am David. I am David. This is me. This is me."

Her silver, high-pitched laugh was as resonant as a bell and as silver as the rest of her.

David could see now that he was in an underground cave, sea green with reflective movements of water.

"There is no point in struggling. You are mine. Mine for ever." Her voice rang out clear as a noise on a clear, frosty day.

"I do not belong to you," said David with rage and hostility. Then he thought guile might serve his purpose better. He subsided into a quiet, fitful mood. There was a chance that he could escape if she undid the weeds tied around his ankles and wrists. There must be some underground passages leading out of the cave.

"I would be grateful if you released the bonds which are digging deeply into my skin. They hurt. I promise you I will not attempt to escape." All the time he had his fingers crossed, so he wasn't really telling a lie.

She laughed with that silvery peal which echoed around the underground cave. "There's no chance of that," she said. "There is no escape from here. Your days of freedom are over."

He watched with attentive eyes as she loosened the bonds tying his arms and legs together. Her presence seemed to ooze around him, to possess, own him. He was a non-entity, a non-person in his own right, an extension of her. He felt like an amputated arm without attachment or use. He was under her spell. She had no need of bonds to restrain him, he was slave to her hypnotic eyes, the wave-like movement of her long hair, when she was present he could not go against her wishes.

It was in sleep that her grip over him seemed to lessen. He would awake calm and resourceful. The apathy and acceptance of his condition had grown less. It was as though his mind was working on his problems, giving him new initiative and encouragement to action. He had a plan and he was eager to put it into effect.

He knew there must be a way out through underground openings to the surface. Unfortunately, he hated narrow passages and low-roofed tunnels. They made him feel claustrophobic and shut in. He felt he could not breathe and that he would never get out to the surface. He had been pot holing when he was younger with a group he belonged to and he had sworn that he would never again go caving. He hadn't told anyone but had kept it to himself. Thinking about it was not going to help. He needed all his resources. To limit himself by thinking negatively would do no good.

The other alternative was to swim underwater, through the seawater filled passages to the pool, the pool where she had lured him into her world, but she'd already guessed that he may consider doing this and with a shrill call had summoned two large sharks with rows of evil teeth around their slit, stretched mouths.

"Contest with them and there won't be much of you left. You will then lose your life and I will lose your companionship. Think before you do anything rash or without thought it could lead to dire consequences which cannot be undone."

David felt leaden with disappointment. What could he do? He had somehow to get out of her clutches, to break free of her domination. He had seen an opening at the back of the cave and it was through this opening that she disappeared at regular intervals during the day. She had a fixed routine. It was at these times that he must make the attempt to get out. He had managed to dull her watchfulness by showing no fight or desire to leave her. He pretended that he was content that he did not want to get out. All the time he was planning, planning, scheming and watching what she did. He knew that it was going to be difficult. He had an inborn fear of caving. He could get lost in a maze of underground passages. He remembered a story he had read about the use of string that would be a guide back to where they had started, but he didn't have any string. He could undo his jumper and use the wool. The whole thing was a gamble.

He meanwhile pretended to accept his captivity and sat apathetically looking into the distance. He longed for the company of someone he was friendly with, someone who could ease his loneliness.

He continued to assess what the Silver Queen did. Only at one time did she leave him alone for any length of time and that was late in the day. It was then that he had to escape. He must put his plan into operation as soon as possible while she was away.

Next day, as soon as she had disappeared, he climbed resolutely to a large opening at the side of the cave. The sides of the cave were smooth walled as though worn even by the continuous movement of water against its hard surface. The going was easy and David's spirits lifted. Perhaps, after all, the difficulties were less than anticipated. They were more in the mind than fact. He whistled quietly to himself.

Then the tunnel started to narrow and become less high. At first, David knelt and crawled along on all fours. Then, he had to lie on his stomach and, reptilian-like, slither along on his belly. There was a fetid, disagreeable odour that made his nostrils wrinkle with disgust. He tried to stop breathing, to avoid inhaling the smell, but this started to make him feel shut in, enclosed, and his breathing became rapid, irregular and distressed and a claustrophobic pressure weighed down upon him. There were tons of earth between him and the outer world.

Then he found that he was wedged, unable to move in the enclosed space. He felt a stifling fear well up inside him and he thrashed out to free himself at all costs. He tried to control the panic but it was only exhaustion that stopped the frantic movements. David realised that it was doing him no good. His hands were wet and sticky, painful and sore and it was blood that ran down his arms. It was warm and it had a salty taste.

He was registering all this through his panic and another thought came to the forefront of his mind. If he concentrated on his breathing, inhaled, held for a short time and then exhaled slowly his surroundings would not cause him so much panic. He couldn't concentrate on his breathing and panic at the same time. He closed his eyes and watched his chest going up and down slowly and still slower and slower in his mind's eye.

Gradually he began to fell more in control of the situation.

Above him was a cavern. It was wide, like a balloon stopper to a bottle. He was wedged in the neck of the bottle. He wriggled first one-way and then another. It was just possible that he could ease his body through by engaging a narrower measurement. With a gasp of relief he realised that the tactic was paying off. He eased his hips sideward. If he could get that measurement fractionally less he would be through.

He had a sudden absurd picture of Pooh Bear stuck in a rabbit hole and having to wait until he was thinner before he could get out. Laughing at the absurdity of it helped. He heard the suction plop like sound as he heaved his trailing legs into the upper cavern. He was free.

There had to be a way out in this direction. He couldn't stand the thought of going back the way he had come. Negotiating the narrow bottleneck again. The fetid smell became stronger and then to his horror masses of moving bodies hurled themselves at him.

He felt overcome with fear as he brushed the bats, because that was what they were, from his face. They were loathsome. The feel of their soft bodies was horrid. But then they were gone and he struggled resolutely on. It was the suddenness of their approach that had thrown him off balance.

The feel of air fanned upon his face, fresh air. He could not believe it. There must be a way out, some contact with the upper atmosphere.

The darkness had lightened to a dim greyness. He was sure now that he was going in the right direction.

There was something coming towards him. He stopped and listened attentively for sounds of movement. There was something out there.

David could make out the shape of something moving along the tunnel to where he was standing. It stood out silhouetted against the lighter background. There was the brush of movement.

David stiffened into rigid immobility. He held his breath and listened fearfully to the noisy pumping of blood through his blood vessels. He hoped that it could not be heard because if it sounded as loud as it did to him, they would be bound to realise that he was there.

The being drew closer and then passed so near that David felt the hot breath in the air. David relaxed and his breath came out in an explosive sound of relief. Whatever had passed had been within a foot of where he was standing. The sound of movement dwindled into the distance and then total silence settled over the area.

Could the Silver Queen have found out about his escape? It was quite probable she may well have returned to the cave and found out that he had gone. He pictured the anger she would show and the threat of what she would do to him if he were recaptured. It did not bear thinking about. He had witnessed several of her angry outbursts while in captivity and the thought of what she could do when thwarted was frightening in the extreme. He cringed with fear, but she hadn't recaptured him and he had no intention of allowing her to catch up with him. He was free and he intended to stay that way.

David made his way carefully towards the glimmer of grey light indicating there must be a way out. If there was anything ahead of him he was prepared and ready to take action.

The light was increasing. The fetid, disagreeable smell was thick in the atmosphere, but there was also a movement of air. David felt it on his face. He felt hopeful. He was going to get out after all, to see the sky up above, and feel the grass beneath his feet. He would be out of this oppressive darkness and in the light again.

There were times when despair had made him give in to the thought that he would never walk among the tall grasses or feel the sun on his skin again. That he would never see the people he loved.

Then the narrow passage opened out into a wide cavern. There was the flicker of light movements as though a fire was burning. David peered through a gap in the flank of rock.

An eerie sight met his eyes. The flickering light from a log fire showed the shape of a green man. He had slits on the side of his neck and a fin-like extrusion along the backbone. His feet were joined together in a webbed fashion and his hands were webbed in the same way, but the upper bones that joined his hands to his body were stunted and short.

He was sitting down some distance from the fire fashioning a tool, the tip of which he was dipping in a silver coloured liquid made runny by the heat of the fire. It was noticeable that he did not like fire or heat because he had draped around him large clumps and strands of seaweed type material, which shielded him from the heat. He had constructed a cascade of water that kept the substance wet. Periodically, he left what he was doing and dived deeply into a pool of water and dipped and came to the surface in a graceful angled movement. He seemed more at home in this environment and had lost that clumsiness of movement that he had when on dry land.

An amphibian thought David.

So intent was he on what he was watching that David stepped backward, lost his footing and caused a cascade of stones to fall into the cave. The creature surfaced from under the water and dragged himself on to the floor that was covered with sand and a conglomerate of stones and gravel. He stood for a second or so, head on one side warily observing the part of the cave where the landslide had happened. He grunted in an alarmed fashion and advanced aggressively towards where David was hidden.

From what David had observed, he showed intelligent behaviour. He was ugly. The warty, thickened skin, the protuberant eyes and the disgusting smell, like rotting fish made David heave as though he was about to vomit.

The creature came closer.

They eyed each other.

A sharp claw lunged out at David. He drew back quickly and it narrowly missed contact with his upper body. David recoiled as the claw came at him again and again.

The grunting increased in intensity.

The creature stopped advancing and eyed his quarry with a malevolent glare from the protuberant eyes. Then he came back to the attack spitting and grunting as he boxed with his claw like talons.

David was being driven across the surface of the cave. The creature advanced purposefully forward. David could feel the heat of the fire on his body. A spark landed on his bare flesh. David winced and tried to rub the area.

The creature kept on advancing towards him as though he had some plan in mind. David knew he had to take some action, to take charge of the situation. He caught hold of a brand of burning wood and thrust it repeatedly at the creature. It drew back in a startled fashion from the heat and flame and hunched its body in a protective way. David thrust the stick fractionally closer and the thing screeched in an eerie manner, shielding his eyes and making frightened, guttural noises. It crouched in the corner of the cave and had lost all his assertive dominance.

David backed towards the entrance of the cave, guessing the direction by the light. He'd already noticed a heap of wood and sticks stocked in the cave. These he dragged over to the entrance blocking it with the wooden logs, driftwood and dried seaweed. Then he thrust the smoking brand on to the dried wood and fled. The smoke swept densely from the smouldering heap and then flames crept upward.

David ran.

This would temporarily stop the creature from following him.

The frightened shrieks of the green fish man echoed around the cave and rebounded back from the side tunnels through which David had so recently passed. The dense, thick smoke made David cough and his eyes burnt and stung. Tears ran down his cheeks as the acrid smoke blew into his face.

Then he was outside. He threw himself down on the hot, white sand and lay there trying to catch his breath. The desert stretched as far as the eye could see. There was a haze over the sun but the sand burnt hot against his exposed skin.

Then he heard the flapping of wings growing louder and louder and a sound unlike anything he had heard before drawing closer and closer.

He looked up and the thing was upon him.

A cruel beak caught him piercing through his clothes and grasping his flesh in a pincer movement. The bird flew upward flapping its massive wings. At first David wriggled and tried to break free from the iron grip, but the movement hurt him and he had to bite his lip to stop a cry of pain from coming deep down inside him.

David lapsed into unconsciousness. When he did open his eyes the desert had given way to rocky outcrops that stretched in ridges across the barren landscape. There was no sign of greenery. It was harsh, bleak country.

David winced with pain. There was nothing that he could do at the moment. To struggle was pointless. He might as well conserve his energy until a more appropriate moment.

The wings of the bird beat rhythmically up and down. The monotony of the movement lulled David into a false sense of security. Then the movement abruptly altered and David watched the ground coming closer and closer.

Just as David was bracing himself for a bumpy landing, the bird glided down to a large, twig structure wedged on a narrow ledge where he released David. He was dropped among rough pieces of abrasive wood. They were Blackthorn and Hawthorn and David felt the thorns scratching and piercing through his clothes and into his flesh.

They were high above the sandy, desert area. It stretched on all sides. And over this the bird was king. There was no movement in the vast, open waste. Just undulating stretches of wind shaped sand and stony outcrops of rock.

The bird pushed David with its beak, further and further along the ledge until he was wedged in the corner. David wondered apprehensively what was about to happen.

Nothing happened.

The sharp-eyed bird swooped down swiftly on a small animal. The movement was scarcely perceptible, but nothing moved in the waste and went unnoticed by this keen-eyed creature.

It flew back up on the ledge and the wriggling animal was held in the cruel talon. It tore at the flesh with his hooked beak. It was a sickening sight, to see the lacerated flesh and blood dripping down among the sticks that formed the nest.

David watched through his fingers the gulping movements of the neck as the pieces of raw flesh disappeared down the creature's throat. David had been feeling waves of hunger and his stomach contracted upon itself. He hadn't had anything to eat for a long time. Now he felt sick with disgust at the sight of what he had just seen. He crouched in the corner attempting to make himself as small and inconspicuous as possible. He was constricted with fear.

The dusk started to envelop the area. There was a contradictory sensation of peace and stillness and a feeling of uneasiness associated with the unknown.

He did not have long to reflect.

A raucous cry and the thunder of wings echoed loudly over the darkening landscape. David had heard this before. Terror welled up inside him. He was unable to move. He knew what it was. It brought back the memory of the day when they had lost Emma.

David couldn't even throw himself down from the ledge. He was frozen into immobility. He remembered the noise, the attack, and the cries of the wounded. He had put it into the back of his mind. He did not want to remember the horror of the day. Now it surged to the surface. He remembered the sound of the heavy wing beat and the sound of it was even now in his ears. The rancid, fetid smell was heavy in his nostrils. The memory of the devastation that had met them when they returned to the spot where the

55

attack had taken place. They had come back to look for Emma. The scene that had met their eyes had been horrific, something that was imprinted on his mind forever. Limbs, blood, bits of body on the reddened, blood-drenched ground.

There had been no sign of Emma.

Tears of fear, loneliness and grief coursed down his cheeks at the recollection of the event. In a flash of memory the pictures flashed in sequence through his mind, one after the other.

He was grasped by the beak of the terrifyingly large, dark shape and the darkness and the terror of the night surrounded him. It flew onward with a steady beat of wings into the still night. David had only his thoughts and memories to keep him company.

He imagined that Emma was dead. At one time he had almost hated her. It had been his sense of guilt that had held him back from expressing it. Now he realised theirs had been an ambivalent love-hate relationship, quarrelling and making it up, and now he missed her company with a deep nostalgia. He longed to have her by his side. Then David remembered the brand of wood that he still held in his hand. He was still gripping it defensively. It may come in handy. It was a weapon of sorts. He eased around fractionally. He could if he made an extra effort thrust the stake into the throat of the creature.

They were flying low. In the distance he could just make out the castellated battlements of a building. There was a yellow glow appearing in the sky and the castle, because that was what it looked like, was outlined against the growing light of dawn. The giant bird seemed to be flying in that direction. Gradually losing height, coming down towards the dark, forbidding building.

The time had come. If anything was to be done, the time was now. He could not wait any longer or the chance would be lost. Then David thrust the stake upwards into the throat of the creature. It shrieked and screamed in an agony of pain. David applied as much pressure as he could to the piece of wood, pushing as much thrust as he could behind the effort. The creature tore at the stake shredding wood in the fury of the attack.

It struggled to reach David, arching its neck back as far as it could. David moved one way and then the other in an attempt to avoid the cruel talons and the sharp teeth.

7

Emma felt her strength leaving her, ebbing away. Her limbs were becoming leaden and weighted, her eyelids refused to stay open. Sleep seemed to be overpowering her and it was a painful struggle to keep awake. She kept on drifting into sleep, dozing off.

"In sleep," Kyoto had said, "there is death." Emma knew that she had to get her circulation moving. She could feel nothing below her knees. Her legs were leaden and as she went to stand up they refused to take her weight. They collapsed beneath her. She rubbed her legs through her clothing trying to encourage the blood to circulate to the extremities. She moved her legs around vigorously and cramp and pins and needles contorted her as she tried to ease the discomfort by pressing her foot down hard on the ground. It didn't work and she fell to the ground in a heap. She rubbed her legs again and made another attempt to stand up rather gingerly, easing herself into an upright position. It was painful as the circulation returned to her lower limbs. Eventually she managed to move a few steps.

There was a flint in her pocket that was a souvenir that she had picked up in a quarry. She'd always carried it with her, just in case one day it may come in useful. And after many months she had found a use for it. With it she could start a fire and thaw herself out and bring some comfort to Kyoto.

She collected twigs and dried bracken and piled them up in a heap. Then came the difficult part, to get it alight, to get the brushwood to catch fire. A spark settled on a dry piece of bracken and a spiral of smoke fanned upward into the cold air. Emma nurtured it like a delicate child, cupping her hands around it a protective way, and her care was rewarded when the flame spiralled upward. She carefully added dried leaves to the bright heart of the flame.

She drew Kyoto as close to the fire as possible. His face was grey. No movement betrayed that he was alive but Emma massaged the cold fingers and chafed the unscored cheek until pinkness came back to the skin.

It was time she did something.

Her eyes took in the vast waste of ice and snow stretching as far as the eye could see. The trees skeletally outlined against the white sky. Some snow fell from a tree alongside where they were sitting melted by the warmth of the fire.

Then a strange pattern attracted Emma's attention. She got up to see what lay on the white snow. It looked like a pathway stretching as far into the distance as the eye could see.

The pathway was made of fallen insects.

She picked up a dragonfly; the lustre of its wings still remained in death. A striped wasp, a bumble bee still coated with pollen, an iridescent-bodied bluebottle, small fruit flies, cattle flies still bloated with blood, mayflies, gnats, all scattered in a stream like a knitted scarf.

She knew she had to follow it.

She struggled on with renewed vigour and a strong hope that all would be well. She covered the ground more quickly dragging the sledge she had made with Kyoto securely tied on to it so that he would not fall off and cause himself more injury.

She wondered at the insects spattering the white snow. What could have caused the deaths of such a wide species of different insects? It was strange. There must be some explanation. The pathway of fallen insects zigzagged as far into the distance as the eye could see. It was uncanny.

Joan Latty

Emma knew in an instinctive way that in this direction
lay hope. Tired to the point of collapse she staggered on.
Her fingers were numb and clumsy. She could not feel the
creeper that she had twisted into a rope, to pull the sledge on
which Kyoto rested. It fell from her hands. She retrieved it
after a struggle and once more they moved slowly onward.

If this proved to be the wrong direction she had no idea
what she was going to do. Her reserves of energy were
depleting. Every footstep was an enormous effort. Any
small problem and she could not cope, could go no further.

Then Emma realised that the air was warmer on her
cheek, that the snow was changing into slush beneath her
feet, and that there was the steady drip, drip of water from
the overhead branches of the trees, and lumps of snow were
falling to the ground. The insects were becoming more
difficult to pick out among the patches of soil and grass that
burst like spring flowers from among the snow. She saw
swathes of green stretching into the distance.

Emma put her hand up to her head. She felt odd.
Everything was going around in circles. She felt herself
stagger and sway as though she could not keep her balance.
She felt herself falling, falling and then she knew no more.

She was still and impassive on the ground, and too
exhausted to be aware of anything around her.

She opened her eyes to blackness, dark as ebony. She
felt exposed and vulnerable. She wondered in a vague,
bemused kind of way how long she'd been cold and still in
the open. There was the hoot of an owl in the tall, towering
trees.

Where was she?

There was a memory of cold and snow and vast
stretches of grass curving to the green trees contouring the
hillside. Then a low moan reminded her that she was not
alone.

She remembered the journey through the snow with
Kyoto impassive, cold and still on the sledge. Somehow she

had dragged him through the snow and ice. What were their chances now?

It was cold, too cold to be out in the open without cover. There was a low moan from Kyoto. She could see the darkness of his form standing out against the lighter horizon where the sky met the darkness of the ground. He was not far from her. She heard him stirring. He needed warmth and comfort and medical care. She could not understand how he had managed to survive. Any further exposure to the elements and he could die. She would have to find shelter for him where he could rest and be treated for his injuries. They had had no food for some time. She distantly remembered gnawing at a stale piece of bread that she had sucked until it had softened and she was able to swallow it. She had forgotten about food, but now her stomach contracted involuntarily and she felt nauseated and sick.

She crawled in the direction from which the low moan had come.

"Kyoto, Kyoto," she whispered. "Can you hear me?"

Even as she uttered the words the uselessness of it overwhelmed her. She sighed her spirits suddenly sank to zero. Kyoto moaned and Emma saw that he was sitting upright, head in hands. She felt his pain in an intense spasm.

Perhaps it would have been better for him if he'd died back there in the snow. Had she been selfish? Had her desire for company made her not consider the life he had ahead of him?

Then Emma saw something coming towards them, movement in the distance, and lights bobbing up and down. Whatever it was was coming this way, moving towards them.

She crouched as low as she could in the sweet scented, wet grass. Were these newcomers friend or foe? Would they be helpful or harmful? Could she afford to let them go by? Until she knew it was wise to keep quiet. The conflict within her continued to bubble around in her mind. They desperately needed food and attention. She knew there could be a risk if she let the wrong people know that they were lying low in the grass.

Then the choice was taken from her hands. Kyoto gave a low moan. It seemed to be amplified by the darkness. The bobbing lights came to a standstill. They were put out, extinguished and, in the darkness, the reality of where they had been was lost. Was it in that direction or over there? They could be anywhere in the still, black of the night.

Emma tried to keep as still as possible. Her breathing was loud in her ears and her heart bumped in an exaggerated fashion. There were flittering shapes and rustling movements around her. They were being encircled. There was no way out, no means of escape, they were captured.

Then they found Kyoto and they twittered like birds around the sledge on which Kyoto was sitting, immobile and head in hands. Then the twittering mob were around her, pulling at her clothes, feeling her face, the orbits of her eyes, her nostrils, her ears, trying to make sense of these strange objects which they had come upon so unexpectedly. The sounds they made were like the high frequency noises that can be picked up by special microphones in underground caves where bats can be found in large numbers.

Emma stood up. She could no longer stand being handled and felt so intimately by the small creatures. She was frightened and started to sob with fear. Then she was tripped to the ground and lay there unable to get up or put up any resistance to the movements that seemed to swarm all over and around her. They were like ants when the Queen ant leaves the nest on a hot summer's day.

Would she wake up and find herself stapled to the ground.

8

Scan searched the grasslands that stretched to the witched wastes of Orzona, where people were known to mysteriously disappear. Every dip, every curve, he peered into cautiously and where there was no visible danger, investigated more fully. In the dark David could have fallen over an escarpment or taken shelter. There was no indication of what had happened to David. No sign of where he had gone. No footprints, crushed grass or broken branches, no movement, not even the twittering of a bird.

There was almost an enchanted stillness about the whole countryside.

Scan had heard about this oasis in the middle of the countryside and had urged his followers to colonise the area, make it their own, so that when the snow came they could live in comfort. For a short time they had lived in peace and calm.

Beyond that plateau was one of the farmsteads they had taken over and made a centre for their activities. Then, no sooner had they established themselves and become self-supporting, than they disappeared, as though they had never existed. There was no evidence of them having been there at all; no sign of disturbance. Everything was in its right place - the fire burning in the grate, a meal simmering on the stove.

They'd waited and waited for someone to return. It was unreal. Time seemed to have stood still.

There was no evaporation from the meat cooking in the saucepan on the stove. The cakes stayed exactly as they were, risen, and unburnt. The fire stayed bright without any need to place wood on it.

It was eerie and no one would stay there for any length of time. Fear drove them from comfort and security.

Scan looked at the tired men around him. They feared the place and it registered on their faces.

"Shall we rest here for the night?" said Scan.

"There is little option," said another man. "I do not like it but there is snow behind and darkness ahead. If we push on we will lose contact with the others and never see them again."

Scan thought of Emma and the hope he'd had that with her help they would overcome the evil in the land. In the short time he had known her, he had become increasingly fond of the red haired girl with the vibrant brown eyes. There was always a smile on her face.

Scan his hopes dashed remembered her with the dull ache of loss and misery. An intolerable despair overwhelmed him with heaviness and the tears flowed down his cheeks. For a short time he had felt hope. Now this hope was dashed. On consideration, he had been wrong to encourage her to leave the land where she belonged. She had been resolute and strong. It must have been painful to leave her family behind and put herself in danger for the sake of Scan and his people.

Then he reassured himself that he had not made her go with any show of force. She had wanted to free them from bondage and slavery. This heartened him somewhat and took away some of the sting and smart of guilt which had settled over him since her loss. He grieved for her with a love that had always known her and a separation that made him feel inner pain.

They crossed the area of land that surrounded the homestead. It was in a perfect state of repair, fences intact and gates oiled and the roof and outside of the building was in good order without a sign of anything needing to be repaired or renovated. It was a haven for the traveller; a roof overhead; food and warmth.

It was an uneasy rest. It was as though they were in a dream world, not in charge of their destiny. They were being manipulated, used, and watched. They felt as though whatever movement or action they made was at the command, the will of someone else. They were like puppets being pulled hither and thither by strings in another person's hands.

They were not in charge of what they did or what could happen in the future.

"We must leave as soon as possible," said Scan. "This place is a place of sorcery, of hypnotic magic. Do you sleep soundly when you close your eyes?"

"Yes," chorused the men together. One man added "But it is a sleep of weird fancies and strange dreams. It is as though something is pulling me towards it. It holds you like being on a magnetic conveyor belt or being drawn along by the pull of a strong current. Then I am frightened by horrific pictures that come vividly into my mind. Distortions of shape, amoebic-like movements that dart out protrusions like fingers that infringe and envelope. The colours are harsh and discordant. Purple, orange and cerise flash and change colour in rapid sequence until my vision is blurred and distorted and not registering what is in front of it. It is like when you rub your eyes and then get flashes of light, similar to exaggerated disco lighting about six to twelve inches from your eyes."

"That's right," said another man.

"And that mocking laughter, peal after peal, an echo in an empty cavern," chimed in another person.

"One peal after the other until the sense of hearing is distorted as well as sight and fear floods through you and panic takes over."

"You've felt like this as well as me," said Scan. "That is my reaction. I have been waiting for someone else to confirm that they are feeling the same way. I did not want to autosuggest and frighten anybody. I see now that it is essential that we get out of this place."

There was a movement among the men.

"We will sleep under the cold, clear stars, under the inverted night sky which seems to come around you like the rounded sides of a bowl. We can breathe the cold night air and inhale energy into our dream-laden brains. Collect your things and we will be away. I feel seaweed in my hair, and the movement of water under my limbs and reeds dragging at my tired body, pulling me under to destruction. I feel as though something is going to happen if we do not get away. There is little time left, of that I am sure. Let us up and away before we are caught like a fish in a net. Quick!"

This urgency seemed to be pathological. This obsession with escape, of getting away. There seemed to be no basis for the extreme forebodings that threatened his existence.

"Let us run, get away before it is too late."

"Why?" questioned another man. "It is so peaceful. The meal will soon be ready and the fire is warm." The man put out his hands to the warmth of the fire, and then his eyes closed, seemed to be lapsing into sleep. Scan shook him vigorously and dragged him into an upright position.

"We must go," he said.

The man grumbled and a flash of anger showed on his fire reddened face. "For goodness sake, leave me, Scan. I choose to stay here where it is comfortable and warm."

Scan summoned all the strength he could in order to stay sane and in charge of his life. The dream-like pull seemed to be saturating his personality. It took all his willpower to focus on his friend and to blot out all the million and one sensations which pulsated in front of him, drawing his attention away from the knowledge that they were in severe danger and not be persuaded to let go and indulge himself in the needs for warmth and food, for which his body was crying out.

66

It was like being in a rotating drum, being stuck like flies to the side of some fairground show and trying to get down and away before the speed lessened. It seemed impossible to his bemused brain. Had they left it too late?

Scan felt intense fear, fear for his very existence, fear of this power which seemed to limit, to drain his attention and his ability to move his body away from where he was being held against his will. He struggled to mentally charge his body to walk, to stride away from where it was, through the door and out into the night.

Then the power increased in intensity, becoming stronger and more dominant. The force dragged at his eardrums, like the magnified beating of hearts out of sequence so that sound impinged on his senses in irregular waves that seemed to grow more powerful, and more powerful by the minute.

He felt as though all his strength was ebbing away, but insistently his mind tried to ignore the peripheral sensations which surrounded his body and to order, command it to do as it was told and to reach out for safety, for the green fields and the dark night sky. The need to rest, to sleep was impinging on his senses in irregular waves which were becoming more insistent and intrusive.

9

Emma listened apprehensively to the twittering noise that surrounded her. The Tom Thumb height creatures were everywhere, examining, feeling, touching. Then she was lifted and carried. The journey seemed interminable, seemed to go on forever. They did not hurt her. Their movements were gentle and they did not jolt or bump her. Emma found herself dozing fitfully, reawakening and dozing off again.

They had draped something soft over her and this made her warm and comfortable. She felt the sleepiness difficult to ward off. Then she knew no more.

She awoke to the movement of water; the back and forward swell on a boat as though at sea. Above was the sky, a velvety blue with a hum of gold on the horizon. They must have recognised that she was awake, because they came to her, opening their arms in a gratuitous manner, assuring her that all was well.

"Kyoto," she murmured, remembering instantly the trek across the snow with the wounded man. They pointed at a still figure, lying not far from where she was.

"He is well," they answered her unspoken question. "He will awake remembering the past as a bad dream."

"But his eye," she stammered and the recollected fear made her struggle and scream out as she remembered the attack of the huge, bat creatures. A convulsion of horror and disgust had broken over her.

"He will be well."

"How can that be?" Emma moaned in a frenzy of despair. "He was horribly disfigured," and a picture came into her mind of the trammelled, claw-scarred face.

They just smiled at her in a soothing, calm manner. "It is all right."

"All right! How can that be?" said Emma, tears flooding down her face. "Nothing will be all right from this day on, of that I am sure. I am lost, do not know where I am," and a wave of self-pity and grief burst over her. She would never see her parents and school friends again. David had got separated from her in this strange world where the prehistoric linked in with the present. Everything was like a bad dream from which she couldn't wake up. The mission that Scan had made out to be so important would never be fulfilled. It was all a fantasy from which eventually she would break free. She longed to see the people she had known when she was growing up. They all seemed to take each other for granted but they were always there when there was a need, supportive and caring.

The small man said, "Trust us. All will be well, of this I am sure. All will be well. Everything is all right, all right," and their small, lithe fingers soothed the pain from her mind, untensed her taut limbs and eased the knots from her tense muscles, until she felt at ease and the frown on her brow relaxed. The tears flowed more quietly, the sobbing which seemed to tear her body apart eased and then stopped. She felt that tomorrow might bring new hope and a change for the better in her circumstances. There was nothing in this moment in time to worry about.

The gentle fingers smoothed her temples and eyelids. She felt relaxed, comfortable and at peace. The sorrow and mourning trickled from her brain and she slept a dreamless, renewing, healing sleep.

She awoke fresh and invigorated, with a resilient knowledge that she would have the strength and ability to face and deal with the difficulties ahead.

"Kyoto," she looked in disbelief at the healed side of his face, fingering the soft pink skin as though she could not grasp what was in front of her. Scarcely a scar showed. The area was clear and smooth. The eye was in the socket and moving normally as though nothing had happened. Emma blinked her eyes and rubbed them to make sure what she was seeing was factual and not in the imagination. She flung her arms around him. "I am so glad," she said. "So glad," and she hugged him to her.

"Are you all right?" he said. "I have been watching over you while you have been asleep. You have shown great courage in the face of adversity. You fought your way through the snow and ice taking me with you, even though I could not contribute or help you out in any way. For this I am grateful even though there were times when I wanted to give up, to beg you to leave me by the wayside, to let me give up. The pain was so bad and the cold seemed to make it worse. There were times when I wished my life was over and that you would let me be."

"Something seemed to drive me on," said Emma. "Even though you were unresponsive for the major part of the time. You were there, by my side, and when I wanted to give up, your being there and needing help was an incentive to keep going." She laughed in a self-conscious way. "There was nothing heroic in what I did. Anyone would have done the same thing under the circumstances."

"I'm not so sure about that," Kyoto said. "But I survived and I am here by your side."

An elfin figure came into the cave-moulded structure they were in. It was built of a polystyrene material, smoothed so finely, it was as though water or larva had surged through the rounded hollow and opened it out in circular shapes, which were womb like and without edges and lit by subtle lighting.

The elfin figure held in his hands a platter of fruit, red skinned apples with a gloss in which you could almost see your face, oranges, peaches, nectarines, grapes and tropical fruit that they rarely saw on the shelves of the supermarket, a gourd of goat's milk, and ripe, sweet scented cheese. He smiled at them and handed the platter to them.

"For you," and his rounded cheeks were almost as rosy as the apples placed so temptingly on the metal plate. His eyes fell before the interested gaze that greeted him.

Kyoto took the tray from him. "It looks good," he said and took an apple and bit deeply into the crisp flesh. In between bites Kyoto spoke to the man.

"Have you always lived in this part of the world?"

The man answered in a secretive, evasive way. "We are here but not here."

"That's a strange thing to say," said Emma. "How can that be? Please explain what you mean," she said in an irritated, manner.

"We live in another dimension, another plane of existence. It is difficult for you to understand how this can be, but it is true, you will have to believe what we say."

Emma felt a sense of confusion, her mind would not register what had been said to her. It did not make sense. Her identity felt fragile and insubstantial. "Am I here?" she said in a doubtful, questioning manner.

"As here as anybody can be," said the man in answer to her question. "It's like lifting a curtain, coming through a black hole from one existence to another. We look substantial, but we are fragile and flimsy figures. We take on the identity and form most suited to whom we are speaking." He interjected helpfully, "We adapt to what you want to see, and our energy fields are versatile and malleable."

"I don't really understand," said Emma plaintively.

"Perhaps, one day you will," replied the man patiently.

"But you are able to restore what is damaged, restore to health those who are broken and ill," said Kyoto with wonder in his voice. "I am an example of your power."

"Be joyful and accepting of what has happened to you and in those quiet moments, ponder on the wonder of it.

71

You are well and you have taken part in something which will always remain a source of incredulity and wonder."

"I know who you are," said Kyoto. "You are the guardians who overlook the universe and bring balance and good into the dark areas where wickedness and evil struggle to assert control." Kyoto humbly dropped his eyes. "I am privileged to have met you. We are followers of Scan and we are on a mission to bring good back to Thanbodia. We ask for your blessing on what we are about to do."

"This I give freely. We are aware of what you hope to do and we know that your party has become separated. You have been driven apart, but you will meet up again. Eventually you will get back together to fulfil what is written in the stars." He smiled at them enigmatically. "They fear for your safety. We have tried to transfer into their minds the thought that you are alive and well. Meanwhile, you must rest here. There is danger abroad and it would be wise to allow the present situation to pass before you resume your journey." He hesitated for a moment. "Rest will increase your resources of energy, and you will face what is ahead with greater resilience. Get to know us. This, for the time being, is your home. We are glad to have you among us." He put his hand up in almost a priest-like manner. "Love and joy be with you and the blessings of this house rest with you."

It was like a benediction, a blessing that left them with an overwhelming sensation of peace.

They lay back among the polystyrene cushions and ate and slept. Their critical faculties and their sense of urgency seemed dulled into insignificance. All was well - all was peaceful. They could allow themselves the indulgence of the warm corner, safety from fear and child-like dependence.

They wandered at will along the subterranean passages lit with a strange, soft glow. There were many wonders to absorb and gaze at around them. It was a foetal life. The roundness of the tunnels and rooms, the pulsating light which was soft and filtered gave them confidence. There was no great outside, only the persuasive inside stretching away, tunnel after tunnel, rounded, hollowed room-like structures, one after the other, in which all the necessities of everyday life were compressed. They had only to wish for music and soft, sultry tones evaporated, crested and crescendoed and then dwindled into nothingness.

It was a hypnotic security that lulled them into an accepting, peaceful state. They no sooner thought of food than generous platters of health giving dishes were brought to them with simple pleasure and the desire to please. Whatever they could wish for was there at a mere request and not a verbal one, thought Emma. In a haze of indulgent security the harshness of the outside world evaporated from her thoughts. She gazed at the orchards, trees growing in the warm, polystyrene atmosphere, polystyrene soil, and marvelled at the ease of their existence. Emma pulled a plum from a tree. The plum was juicy and sweet, dark and delicious and the juice ran down her fingers.

They had no idea how long this idyllic existence went on.

Emma started to feel uneasy, restless. She wanted to do something for herself. Even by pulling the plum and eating it straight from the tree was an example of the renewed desire that stirred within her for action and independence. It was a spontaneous action, taking that plum from the branch of the tree. It somehow did something to her, made her feel invigorated and full of energy and the will to act for herself and not be dependent on those around her for her everyday needs.

Kyoto had been restless for some time. She had sensed this feeling but had abruptly dismissed it from her mind. It seemed strange and unrelated, but after this experience the things that they needed were not so readily available. They had to do things for themselves. This at first annoyed them. They felt badly done by, abandoned, but then they gradually adapted to a more resourceful existence. Gone the polystyrene, foetal life and the replacement sky above and the soil below. They enjoyed the simple pleasure of growing their own vegetables in an accelerated fashion. They seemed to germinate and grow so quickly, thought Emma. Seeds sprang into existence and were ready to eat by teatime. It was a miracle in itself. They prepared aubergine, things that resembled red and green peppers and fruits that were like green bananas but were delicious in their unripe state and had a delicate flavour of their own. These were prepared in exotic ways that tempted their taste buds and made eating a pleasure.

Then came the day when they were summoned to the council. The guardians felt the time had come to face the world. To go back to where they had left off. The room the guardians were in was psychedelic. A pulsating glow of strong primary colours that vibrated and changed consistently. Emma tried an experiment. She forced her mind to concentrate on a mellow, torpid scene, golden under the Autumn sun and as though by magic the scene in front of her changed. Immediately she thought of snow-laden branches, ten feet drifts across wide motorways, and ice floes on the rivers and in front of her was all that she had pictured.

She grinned putting herself more enthusiastically into the game. The guardians sitting sedately at an oblong boardroom table changed into frog-like creatures, sitting on lily pads and croaking incessantly. Then they changed into chimpanzees having a tea party, mouthing and jumping up and down.

"You have found us out," said one of the guardians. "We are amoebic in character and can flow into whatever your mind pictures. You think and see what you want to see."

"It's fun," said Emma.

They smiled indulgently at her. "We hope you are rested.

The time has come to go forward on your mission. We will send a group of our people to see you safely on your way. You will travel under the coat of their invisibility. Take heart," they said in response to her apprehensive, fearful expression, "you have no need of us now. You are rested mentally and physically. We are glad to see you so." They smiled at her in a warm, winning way that made Emma feel expansive and comfortable.

"Yes, all good things have to come to an end," sighed Emma. "If only I knew what Scan wants of me. I have no direction or purpose. If only our paths had not separated."

"Do not be fearful. You will find an answer in times of difficulty through a sign, a person, something you read or from deep inside you. You will not lack direction when the time of need is evident. There is no need to be fearful. Have faith and know all will be well. You will have many people around you who will give you strength. My love and a kiss of peace, support you in times of danger and stress. Peace be with you, joy be with you, love be with you always. May all that is good protect you from all that is harmful." With these words they disappeared and Emma and Kyoto found themselves on the green, sorrel-covered plains, the golden gorse permeating the air with a warm, coconut fragrance. There was a warm balm about the air which made Emma feel relaxed and tired as she used to on those first, early Spring days in her own country.

10

Scan awoke in a bemused, questioning, torpid sort of way. He had no idea where he was. Around him were tall trees. He was lying on a springy bed of pine needles, the warm smell of pine resin on the damp, misty air. Not far from him were his companions. Vague recollections stirred within him. He dimly remembered the spell-like power that had impinged on his senses with a strength and urgency more overwhelming than anything he had known or experienced. It flooded his mind with slide after slide of pictures, like a reel unrolling one after the other.

The power had gone. But what had happened? How had he and his companions got away? He felt drained of energy as though a fierce battle had taken place. Scan knew this to be true. It had been on the psychic plane. He had held his own. He must have or they would not be where they were now. He had fought off the evil influences that had threatened to engulf them.

He and his companions were free. Relief flooded through him as he breathed in deeply the pine scented, moist wood air. They were free, free as the bird that was flying overhead. He roughly shook his companions into consciousness.

"You are free. Breathe in deeply the clear air of freedom. Draw it into your lungs to dispel the lingering fantasies that tortured your brain. Breathe the sweet scented air into your sleep bemused brains and be grateful that you have not been absorbed, disintegrated from that which you are, into the Sea Witch's submissive slaves. She almost lured us into her seaweed-draped, barnacle-encrusted surroundings.

"We are free. The power of her spell has been broken by our defiant stand in the face of her tyrannical strength. Her dominion in this place is over. No longer will the fire burn without new wood, the kettle boil on the hob, and soup simmer on the stove. Her spell is broken and will no longer be a threat to the traveller. We could live here in peace if we so wish. This I know to be true. All is well." Scan completed his comment and sat back in a relaxed, contented way and let out a long drawn sigh of relief.

"On what basis do you hold this opinion?" said a depressed, pessimistic character that had all along cast a negative influence over the group. "You have no grounds for this optimism."

"I know from deep down inside myself," said Scan. "Even your niggling doubts do not alter one whit the conviction that I know to be true." An air of finality showed upon his face. "Come, let us move on. We are wasting time in argument."

The other man was not going to give up and accept this statement without a fight. "More substantiation is what I require."

"What proof do you want?" said Scan impatiently.

"For a start let us go back to the house. You say the magic is broken. In that case, let us wait and spend the night there."

The other men drew back in fear.

"No! There's no way I'll go back there."

"Nor me neither. I'd rather sleep under the stars in the cool, clear night air."

"There is nothing to fear," said Scan reassuringly. "I would be quite prepared to forget what has happened here and move on, but to prove the point we'll go back to the homestead." He turned in the direction of the smallholding in a purposeful manner. The others dragged behind like reluctant children dawdling on their way to school. Obvious apprehension showed on their faces as they drew closer to the high hedge surrounding the building. It had grown taller and more bushy and uncontrolled. The pathway to the house was nearly lost in a sea of tall grasses and weeds and they had to push against it to get in through the gate. The door to the house was stiff and one of the hinges came off from the frame when it was pushed hard to open. It gave way with a squeaking of rust and a piece of wood fell off the side of the door on to the ground. It was rotten and riddled with beetle holes.

The room was cold, unfriendly and unwelcoming. No fire burned in the grate. No soup steamed on the hob. The cold ashes were scattered around the fireplace. Dust was thick on the table and litter was scattered over the floor.

"Are you satisfied?" said Scan. "The spell is broken."

"You stay here at your peril," said one of the men entering the room. "Never again would I rest peacefully in this house. You may tell me that the spell is broken but I never want to run the risk of remaining in this place." He brushed down a cobweb that dangled from an overhanging beam.

A mouse ran across the room and disappeared down a hole in the floorboards.

Even Scan shivered involuntarily. "Come, let us go," he said.

An overwhelming sense of peace came over him as they stood outside the wind fresh in their faces. "On, to Tingate Well," said Scan. "I feel the evil that has afflicted us and this land of ours will be a thing of the past. I have a firm conviction that all will be well."

"Once again you have no foundation for this hope," said the pessimist, a cock's feather stuck jauntily in the ribbon around his cap. "I am appointed leader and I say we must go back. You are not allowed to make decisions without a democratic vote. You take too much on your shoulders. I suggest we make our way back along the route we have followed and live in peace under the power of Xylo." The man went on talking. "He is good. He does no harm or hurt. His way is peace."

A disgruntled grumbling came from the rest of the people.

"We want peace. We are tired of this quest, the hardship, the discomfort and the continual sense of getting nowhere. We want a vote. We want a vote."

They lifted their hands and shook them in time to the words. Scan felt oppressed by this formidable opposition. He felt intuitively that the enemy had infiltrated this man. It was all very well to be strong but in this case strength was in numbers. One or two dedicated individuals could do little. Their numbers had already been decimated by what had happened en route.

"It is your right to speak and be heard," said Scan.

An insect, resembling a bee hovered fractionally above the party. Hovered and then darted as though something had attracted its attention. Scan watched it, half attentively, in an abstracted manner, his eyes drawn to the clown-like antics. Was there something more sinister about the sequence of movements? It seemed to be keeping in line with Gump, the man who had provoked the incident. As Gump moved it did also.

"You have no need to fear Scan. He is not God Almighty."

Gump turned in another direction and the hovering insect with iridescent, dragonfly wings darted around in the direction that Gump was facing. This was away from Scan. Scan speculatively put his finger to his chin. An experiment, he must try this out.

"I do not wish to make you fearful," he said. "I have never forced you to do anything. At all times I have respected your opinion and there has been no coercion. We have done things together willingly, it was a joint choice. I do not believe in tyranny or manipulation to get my own way. We have worked together and of this I am glad."

Gump turned, hate mirrored on his face. "You drive with uncanny compulsion."

The insect darted around to the front of Gump and hovered in line with his forehead.

"You get the men to follow you so that, even though I do not believe in your methods, I have no alternative but to do as you say. There must be others who feel the same."

"Perhaps, but in my case, that is not true. I follow Scan because what he has said in the past has been proved to be true and to all our advantage," answered a man behind Gump.

Gump spun around to the direction of the voice and the insect spiralled around into a frontal position.

"You can always go it alone."

"That's true," said another voice.

"I'm not sure that I want to follow you. Scan has taken us through many perilous adventures. He has always in the past had my confidence. Nobody has complained before."

Gump mumbled incoherently to himself then added "That may be, but situations and attitudes change."

"Got it," said Scan, swatting the empty in air a mysterious, unexplained fashion.

"Got what?"

Scan picked up the iridescent insect writhing in death and put it out of its agony with a downward movement of his heel on a large outcrop of stone. Mystified, the others watched, surprised at this unusual behaviour, because Scan had always shown a respect for other life forms and was reluctant to kill without cause.

Gump had stopped talking. His mouth, which had been vociferously yelling abuse at Scan and broadcasting his shortcomings, stayed in an open, death position. His eyes were glazed and staring.

"What has happened to Gump?" said one man moving

towards his still, rigid body.

"Stay!" said Scan. "He is not one of us."

"Not one of us?" repeated the man.

"I have known him since childhood," said one of the older men. "He has lived alongside me. He was one of Red Runcorn who tilled the fields in Sol."

"That may be so," said Scan. "But this man is not Gump."

There was further mumbling and movement in the crowd. "What Gump said is true. Scan is not fit to lead us. He is ailing and ill."

"He does not recognise Gump," said one man in a dazed, questioning way.

"There must be something wrong with him," said another. "We all know Gump."

They turned towards the stricken figure that now lay on the grass in a decomposed, dead manner. The flesh was falling off his bones in an accelerated fashion. They turned in disbelief to Scan.

"What is happening? This is sorcery, witchcraft, and evil. Let us away. There is no point in staying." Pure fear registered on their faces and Scan knew that if he didn't gain their attention and confidence they would scatter, and turn tail and run.

"Wait! There is no need to panic and run off. We must pull together. We can do nothing unless we do it as one."

Scan followed the direction of the men's attentive eyes to where Gump's skeletal form was stretched out on the grass.

"Yes, I knew Gump, but not this travesty of Gump. Gump was a brave, good man. He thought for himself and had a conscience which made him follow right." He assessed the bewilderment on the watching faces of the men. "This is not Gump." He waited for the statement to sink in.

Again the ripple of disturbance carried over to him, like

along a vibrating wire.

Not Gump, not Gump, not Gump. It looked like Gump. If it wasn't Gump who was it?

Then he felt their attention coming back to him. He waited until the full force of their mind power was focussed on him. Then he said, "This was a travesty of Gump. He was in the power of Xylo."

Again the bumbling of minds. "Power of Xylo, Power of Xylo, Power of Xylo."

And then the attention came back to him again. "The real Gump is dead. The Gump who was always courageous, brave and astute was no more in this decayed shell."

The shocked look was still on the faces of the men as they looked at the desiccated bones of the man, Gump whom they had loved. They seemed paralysed into inaction by the findings they had made.

"Gump was a clone, a copy of the Gump that we lived alongside. He must, at some time, have been overwhelmed by the power of Xylo. It can happen all too easily and, once captured, they are no longer the person they were. They lose their real, true identity. They become slaves to Xylo and nothing deflects them from that purpose. They have no loyalty or remembrance of those they once loved. They cannot discriminate between right and wrong. They look like the real person they were, but that is as far as it goes. They are an empty shell, a replica, and a copy. Gump was in the power of Xylo." He hesitated for a moment. "The insect I killed was acting as a message conductor, an extension of the false Gump. A control that kept Gump in contact with Xylo. He was linked in as though through a telephone system. That insect with dragonfly wings was not what it appeared to be. It was rooted in evil. As soon as I swatted the insect, Gump was immobilised. Do not mourn for this." He kicked the bones with a disdainful, distasteful look on his face.

The men looked alarmed, shocked at this sacrilege.

"Mourn and remember the Gump that used to be.

Remember his loyalty, his belief in the rights of the individual, his love for his fellow men."

Sorrow and tears showed on their faces.

"His spirit will live forever, do not fear for him. His good goes before him and his knowledge remains a help to us in times of difficulty."

Comfort registered on the faces of the men who were listening to what Scan said.

Scan continued with scarce a break. "We must move on. Make up time."

The men accepted Scan's leadership without dissension or argument.

"What chance do you think we will have?" said one of the men in a grave, serious manner.

"I have an intuitive feeling all will be well. Something deep inside me makes me feel strong and hopeful. Even if we do not all survive, I am sure enough will get through to make victory certain. Come, there is no time to stand any longer in the open. We are susceptible to attack. Xylo and his minions will have got a fix on our position. They will know where we are. The transmitter will have seen to that. Our position is perilous."

He made to move off. "Wait! Drag that skeleton." Scan turned toward the ground where the body lay but it had totally disappeared. Grey dust was all that remained and even as he spoke the wind in a whirlpool swirled it upward into the atmosphere. They watched with disbelief as it disintegrated into the distance.

"Let us clear all signs of our being here," said Scan with urgency. "We are in great danger. I hear the sound of the enemy approaching and the beat of their mighty wings getting louder and louder."

Fear reflected clearly on the tense, anxious faces of his followers. They stumbled towards shelter, knowing how important it was to hide from the fearsome sounds of the approaching dense, black cloud of movement.

11

David felt the creature losing height. Down and down it plummeted. David turned the stake he held in his hands with the intention of using it as a weapon, and tried to thrust it home deep within the throat of the bird. The creature tried to attack the pallid, two-legged creature that was causing such intense, excruciating pain. He tried to dislodge and cast the thing down on the rocks below.

Valiantly David held on attempting to avoid the clawed, taloned feet of the infuriated creature. He held on grimly to the wooden stake that was embedded in the throat of the massive bird. There was little David could do. He knew that if he fell it would be to his death. He would not survive.

The rocks and the boulders in the wild terrain stood up harsh and forbidding against the lowering black sky. David realised that he had mistimed the attack. They had been flying too high, and even though they had lost height in the skirmish, the creature seemed to have an inexhaustible supply of energy, which David found incredible, unbelievable.

Blood was pouring from the ugly mouth and dripping down the breast on to the under parts of the bird and a spray of red splattered on David and down to the ground below. Yet the wings of the bird moved rhythmically backwards and forwards and the bird managed to hold its height. The earth appeared a long way beneath them.

David knew that he had to hold on and try to avoid the arching of the impaled neck as the bird with unbelievable courage tried to sink its sharp, needle-like teeth into David's body. He lunged this way and that, frantically trying to avoid those menacing teeth and fangs, because this bird had what looked like fangs in the yawing, oral cavity.

David was tired and his movements were growing slower. A sharp sting made him aware that something had punctured the skin on his thigh and a burning sensation intensified, moved up the limb and then his body. There was no feeling. He could not move. His body was paralysed.

David almost expected to be parcelled up in an arachnoid fashion. Were there spider spinnerets among the feathers? But nothing happened. David struggled to find the faintest sign of movement below the waist, but there was no muscular response to his vain attempts. He was rigid, immobile.

The bird, even though injured, had managed to call upon extra source of energy. Its wings beat resolutely and purposefully as the bird carried its prisoner across the rocky, barren plain.

Where were they going? For what purpose had he been captured? In panic and intensified fear, he watched the rock give way to shrub and bush, and then to the wind-contoured desert again. The heat hit him like a physical blow. He felt nauseated and sick. His body heaved and retched.

David closed his eyes to shut out the visual movement of the ground below keeling and swinging in and out of focus. The brilliant light of the overhead sun, and the abrupt swinging movement jarred his head and neck. It was excruciatingly painful. The sensation above his shoulders seemed to be intensified by his body paralysis. Then he felt himself losing consciousness

He awoke in the fetid, enclosed atmosphere of imprisonment. Light filtered from a grill set high in the wall, but it was not enough to penetrate the dense darkness where David found himself. Underneath, the ground was damp, soft and moist. The smell hit his nostrils, a smell like the fungal breakdown of wood when dry rot is present. The dull moans of other people overcome by despair, misery and desperation made David shiver with fear and apprehension.

He wanted to move on to his side, but however much he struggled he was quite unable to turn from one position to another. Not a muscle in his lower body responded to his attempts. Earlier he had been able to move his head, but now the paralysis had extended and no longer could he make a fractional twitch of movement. He felt terror and panic well up inside him like a filling tidal basin. It was all finished. There was nothing he could do. It was up with him.

Then he remembered the previous time he had felt this despair and depression battening him down. It was on the perilous journey through the underground caverns. This recollection made a spiral of hope surge up inside him. It was not up until he was still and cold. His limbs were warm, he knew that.

It needed time before the drug wore off, for the paralysing effect of the sting to disappear. It was obviously not lethal or he would not be there weighing the situation up. Perhaps, by varying his breathing, the effects would wear off. He could not move, so exercise could not be used to any purpose. Then could he deep breathe? Of course he could otherwise he would not be alive. He knew that deep breathing increased the oxygen to the brain. He had read it somewhere. And by doing this it would eliminate the poison in his system. Resolutely he made himself breath deeply and rhythmically, holding his breath for as long as he could, concentrating totally on what he was doing. It made him feel more together and capable.

Hope danced like magic inside him.

Then a terrifying shriek rent the darkness apart. David held his breath. All physical sound suspended except for the thudding of his heart, which sounded unnaturally loud in his ears. He wanted to identify where the sound came from. The silence was stifling and oppressive. Nothing could be heard but the beating of his heart and the involuntary gasp of indrawn breath, as he could hold it no longer.

All around him was still.

The paralysis was wearing off, so his supposition was right, it was not permanent. It was a temporary condition. He found he could move fractionally. There had been a response when he had attempted to move on to his side. After several abortive attempts, he was on his side instead of straggling on his back like an upturned tortoise. He had managed to turn and then fall back into his original position, as there was not enough muscular strength to complete the movement.

Then someone else shrieked out in abject agony. The sound echoed eerily through the hollow, cavernous structures. David felt the hair stand up in hackles on the back of his neck.

"What was that?" he said to the darkness and was surprised when there was a response to his question.

"They be breaking Tutsin. He was a brave man, always did what was right, never afraid of standing up against the strongest when he felt people were being treated unfairly. That's what got him there, standing up for someone else, never a thought of what could happen. Right was right to him."

There was silence in the cell.

"Isn't it possible to get help to him?" said David.

"Help! You must be joking. This place is as isolated and impregnable as a fortress. Might as well be on an island in a shark-infested sea."

"Where there is life there is hope," said David, trying to bolster his failing courage.

"They don't kill you here," said the man. "They change you from what you are into something with no will of your own. You become like puppets pulled by strings." He sighed and was silent for a short time. "You see people you have grown alongside since childhood become unresponsive, no laughter or tears, cold and their sole meaning in life is a unquestioning obedience to their new master. He is everything to them, nothing else matters, no family, friends, no ideals, no loyalty to anyone other than this obeisance to someone they have never really met in person."

"Who is this Master?" said David in a faltering tone.

"The Wizard of Xylo. He is wicked and powerful."

David cringed back against the damp wall of his prison. What could he do? Tears coursed down his cheeks and sobs wracked his throat.

"Crying are you?" said the man. "There be plenty of that here. No need to hide your tears. Sometimes renewed courage comes when the tears are spent. At this moment in time you are alive. Your heart is beating strongly. Be brave. There must be a way to bring back good into the world. Even as we talk greater powers are at work striving to create balance."

"They will fail," said a quavering, thin voice. "There is no good in the world, that I tell you. Evil is all-powerful. They will fail, fail," and his croaky voice lapsed into silence.

The darkness lapped around David like an impenetrable wall that cut off all else. Then, David saw light growing in intensity as day broke through the grill he had noticed earlier. If there was light then the powers of evil had not taken over the universe. They were not dominant. A wave of new hope ran through him. He could still feel and assess. They could not hurt him or harm him unless he let them, and firmly he set his jaw and chin into a strong line and felt the inner strength burn brightly inside him. "You must have faith in yourself," he said.

Then a hollow shriek echoed once more through the fortress, growing louder and more penetrating, and then fading back into obscurity, and then peaking in another crescendo. 'How can one hold out against this?' he thought, but his spoken words were different.

"Power is universal. It is there for all who are in need. Let us call upon the guardians of the universe to come to our aid."

It was as though someone else was speaking through his vocal chords inspiring confidence. "All will be well. Your condition may be oppressive and depressing but do not let despair blunt your hope. Allow your senses to be sharp and aware like a newly honed knife. Grasp any opportunity when it offers itself and make the most of what is on offer. You may then be able to change the situation that you are in effectively." He hesitated for a moment and then went on. "Even now the paralysis that was affecting my body is passing off, and I can move around a little more than I could a short while ago." He continued in a well-modulated comforting voice. "Do not be fearful. You have those by your side who will give you strength and will comfort and support you in those difficult moments in your life. Believe in their power, strength and love, and know they are always at hand."

There was silence as David finished his words. Then muffled sobs as though his words had had an emotional affect. David felt weakness like icy fingers spread through his body. He had taken charge, but in the darkness it was not known that he was a mere boy, with fear coursing through his veins. What had made him speak like that? It was as though some outside force had him under control. Then panic overwhelmed him. They had him. He was controlled. He was no longer David.

Then there was the grating of a metal key in an unoiled lock and the squeaky hinges of the cell door opened inwards. David saw the flicker of light from outside in the corridor and the heavy tread of feet clumped across the stone floor, a chain clanking behind the shackled legs. Then the shadowy figure fell as though pushed with tremendous force. There were cries of pain as the man fell against other people stretched out on the cold floor.

"It is Tutsin," said a voice.

And yelps of pain rent the air as a leather throng lashed out among them. Again and again it cut into their flesh. David felt the smart and sting as it caught his unprepared body. David felt hate as his body withstood the pain of this undeserved attack. The injustice of it made him burn with resentment. What had he done to deserve this uncalled for attack?

"I have done nothing to provoke your anger. Stop it! Stop it I say."

The whip lashed out again forcibly causing anguish and anger among the men on the floor. All was silent again.

"Tutsin, are you there?" said an inquiring voice.

Silence greeted the question.

"Someone be here," said a harsh, abrasive voice. "He landed square on my belly and as hard as I wriggle to ease him off he sticks like a limpet on a rock."

The effort the man made to shove off what had landed on him showed in the strident character of his breathing. "I can't do it. Here give us a hand, he's like a tonne weight." There was the shuffling of movement. "That's better. He's unconscious, there's not a movement from him."

There was a lull in the conversation.

"It's not knowing when they'll come for you. This endless wait in the damp and dark which gets you down."

Then they heard the heavy approach of footsteps in the outside corridor. David listened with suspended breath. He was hoping the footsteps would go on past, they would get louder and then fainter as they passed the door and went on further down the corridor. But no, there was the rattling of keys and they were among them again with the hard-hitting whip that bit cruelly into their flesh. Rough, hairy arms were searching, feeling, fingering their faces and bodies. Then to David's horror the one examining him said, "Here he be," and he was dragged across the uneven stone floor bumping from one body sprawled on the ground to another on his way to the open door. He was tossed down outside while the key grated in the lock, but this time he was on the other side of the door.

12

The movement of wings became louder and louder and the heat and the oppressiveness thrust upon them. Scan knew as leader all hopes of success lay with him.

"Follow me. There is no time to waste. I know a way that will take us through the Hills of Sidon into the valley of the well. Come there is no time to lose."

They slipped down the scree-covered slopes of the hillside. The sudden movement set off an avalanche of small stones which rattled down on to the people who were in the front of the group and some of them slipped and fell further down the slope, but no one seemed to be seriously injured and they continued down the slope to the floor of the valley. Then they were in the opening of a large, cool cave that led into the hillside. They pressed up against each other with the intention to get in and away from the danger that threatened them. They worked hard and frantically to block the opening to prevent anyone following them into their place of safety.

"Do you know the way?" said one man looking around him with a doubtful look on his face. "I fear underground caverns and the damp darkness. To get lost in the bowels of the earth, to wander aimlessly in deep potholes, to walk alongside clear, deep underground streams that suddenly gush subterraneanly into a deep, bottomless gully. It is not for me."

"Yes, it is a fearsome thought," added another man. "To be under tonnes of stone and earth. It is like being buried alive. I like to see the blue sky above and the green grass below and feel the cool air on my face. Do not take offence. I am a mountain dweller. I think I shall wait until all is quiet outside, then I will climb over the crags and mountains, make my way through the valleys and passes, look down on the countryside stretched out below and feel the cool wind on my face. I climb under the star-studded sky. We will meet again." He hesitated for a moment then added, "Who is for travelling with me?"

Scan felt he was losing his grip. He was losing support. How many would go with Imto? A few drifted uncomfortably to Imto's side.

"Not for me, underground caverns and darkness."

"Nor for me," said another.

A few other men moved to Imto's side encouraged by the movement of the first who had come to a decision.

Scan surveyed the dwindling numbers of his followers. "It must be your decision. The obligation must be to do as you think fit. There is no coercion." Scan shrugged his shoulders as though dismissing the situation.

"Well, you know what it is like," said one man in a guilty, indecisive manner, "We've been together for a long time and it causes me pain to leave your side and go with another."

"There is no disloyalty involved. Each of you must be true to yourself. If you feel something is right for you, follow that inner note and do not be distressed. We will meet again of that I am sure. So, go in peace."

The group parted with much emotion and highly charged feeling. They had been companions for many moons, and it was hard to admit that for the time being their paths split.

"Peace go with you," said Scan, in a benign, loving manner.

"And with you, also," responded the other men. There were tears on the faces of the men as they separated.

"We will meet again to complete the task before us. Never fear!"

The light from the cave entrance grew dimmer and

dimmer as they penetrated deeper and deeper underground.

They gasped in wonder as stalactites hung down from the rugged roof like a curtain and stalagmites mounted, rose like pillars to the roof, interlacing in a pattern. They had never seen anything like it before and they raptly gazed in wonder at what was before them. The scene was lit by an eerie light that flickered from some unknown focus. There was the continual drip, drip of water.

They came to crystal clear water through which they had to wade. It was so cold that it clamped icy fingers around their calves and thighs and caused muscular spasms in their leg muscles. The sights were spectacular. They walked along tunnels which widened out into cathedral shaped caves, where the roof towered high, high above in a trellised, stone pattern worn over many years by the movement of water. They resonated and echoed to the sound of their footsteps and a phosphorescent glow eerily shimmered over the water that was everywhere.

They jumped over gulleys where a dislodged stone fell into the darkness and did not register hitting the bottom of the gap. Sometimes the span was too wide to bridge with a jump and they had to crawl across an outcrop of stone that joined, like a natural bridge, the two parts of the cave, high above a gap that reached down into impenetrable darkness. They climbed the lime-encrusted walls, their hands searching for uneven stones to grip on to, and their feet wildly searching for footholds in the surface of the rock.

They had just negotiated a narrow ledge where one of their number had slipped, and for a moment it appeared as though they were going to lose him in the dark depths that reached far below them. The unfortunate man hung on with muscles straining in his arms, until those alongside him, before the fall, with supreme effort and not without endangering their own lives, pulled him to safety.

They had rested for a short time after this incident. They talked quietly among themselves about the wonders they had seen. It was a world of marvels where something dramatic greeted their sight at each turn of the corner. The rocks shaped themselves naturally into Rodin type sculptures.

It was like the dark patches where paint had peeled off and imaginary patterns tempted the imagination to form strange shapes into known patterns. It kept them awe struck with wonder. Each one lost in his interior world.

Their journey took them along passages glazed and smooth with scarcely a hold to grip their torn fingers into to stay safe. Scan kept their confidence with his firm conviction that they were moving in the right direction. They were not lost. The others thought his body radiated a visible light that glowed and shone from inside him. It held them together like a flame of hope.

They had been underground for so long that they had no idea what length of time had passed since they had first entered the cave opening. They wondered how the men whom had opted for the mountain path were. They knew that there were many dangers in the high mountainous region and in a way, by taking this path; they had avoided the aggressive peoples who lived in that part of the country and were well known for their warlike behaviour.

They were getting used to life underground and they wondered at what held the mountain together. It was a miracle that subsidence did not happen on the surface more often than it did because the interior of the mountain was hollowed out. The cavernous caves and cathedral-like halls flickered with a mysterious, green light, which reflected the stillness in the depths of the ocean. It made them stand awe struck with wonder at the sights before them.

Then they became aware of a strange, unaccountable noise, which vibrated through the tunnel, the hollowed out formation. The noise of motors hummed through the walls. It sounded like a generator, the dull drone of machinery.

There was a glow of light which seemed to swell and

subside and the grind and whirl of movement. Mystified and frightened they stood and listened and wondered what was ahead of them.

"I wish I had gone with Imto," said one. "I prefer the sky up above. I be afeared of demons and hobgoblins and things that live underground."

"You look for hostility where there is no evidence that any exists. You need to keep an open mind and not look for trouble. Let us put our heads together and pool our resources. A lot can be gained by working as a unit. Let us decide what to do."

They huddled together against the glazed wall that seemed to pulsate with warmth and heat and was relaxing and comforting. It eased their tired bodies and seemed to give them an added sense of oneness, unity and purpose.

"I will go ahead," said Scan. "I will be back to let you know what I have found. Take heart. I have a feeling that all will be well and that nothing harmful will happen to us."

Silently he moved away from them. The ground was glazed and sloping downward and Scan slid noiselessly out of sight. It was like being on a giant playground slide. The incline went precipitously downward. There was nothing to grasp or hold on to in order to lessen the speed of the swift descent. Scan's confidence was shattered by the lack of control over the situation. Anything that was about to happen was totally out of his hands. He was powerless to influence his future or do anything to stop what was occurring.

He wished for invisibility and his courage upturned like a rotated hourglass at the thought. If he imagined he would not be seen, then it was possible that it could become a fact. Then, whatever was out there could not intrude or see him. A wave of exhilaration thrilled through him and like a child he almost believed it could be true.

Then, he came to an abrupt halt and what was in front of him was a mystery that he did not understand. Masses of pyramidal shapes made out of glass or clear plastic material covered the entire floor of a massive cave structure, hollowed out in that same smooth, glazed, unmarked manner. It was the colour of malachite, reflecting a sunny greenish blue, like the tropical, paradise island sea where you could see deep into the depths to the coral reefs below and watch the shoals of fish darting and flitting in among the holes in the coral. There was an iridescent gold, gold of autumn in September and October when the blackberries were thick on the brambles, the gold of warmth and mellowness, of mature wine.

In each pyramidal shape there was a humanoid figure sitting cross-legged in a yoga position on the floor. They had large heads and small bodies. They did not stir. As Scan drew nearer he could see the regular pulsating of the pyramidal shape as though in time to respiration, and as Scan registered what was in front of him, a voice echoed with clarity through the cavernous structures.

"What message do you bring to the Valley of the Meditators? Speak!"

Scan picked up the vibration and the meaning of the words. They had recognised that he was there. What powers had these strange people, who sat immobile and seemingly impassive in their pyramidal structures? Which one of the individuals in their cut off worlds had contacted him? There was no sign of visible movement or any indication of which one had spoken.

Scan felt vulnerable and fearful. He felt that buzz of adrenaline which prepares the body in times of danger to turn and run, to flee from a threat, freeze into immobility, or to attack and stand up to the enemy.

"There is no need to be fearful. We mean you no harm. We are peaceful people." There was a brief hesitation and then the voice continued. "Do you bring peace or the sword of discontent and war?"

A glass screen fell before Scan's advancing body and

one fell behind him, so that he was cut off in a double glazed, sectional pocket. He was a prisoner.

"Join in union with us and bring peace where there is war, joy where there is fear." Scan felt no sense of unity. His mind ran anxiously over the experiences of the last few minutes and fretted about the delay that it was causing him. He had no time to sit and meditate. The thoughts flickered in rapid sequence through his mind. Every minute counted. It was imperative that he got out of here and on his way. What could he do to make them see his dilemma? There must be some solution to his problem.

Then he saw ahead of him a monitoring screen and to his abject horror the thoughts that were going through his mind and the emotions he was feeling were displayed prominently before him. He felt empty and exposed, naked without any protection to screen him from the barrage of eyes that viewed him with emotional detachment.

Then, he felt his separateness dwindle, disappear into a void. He struggled against the power that seemed to be swamping his individuality. Then he knew no more of struggle. He felt merged with something that was greater than himself. He felt happiness, fullness, and an outgoing well being that seemed to expand and grow from within him until he felt expansive and large. He could liken it to the radiance around the wick of a candle that flooded out into the area around it in a multi-coloured band of light. He was one with all the other rainbow multi-coloured bands that were expanding and moving outward around him.

He knew a happiness that exceeded anything that he had known before. He yearned to extend his arms and embrace the whole world. The fullness he felt brought total compassion and understanding, a love for all life forms in the universe. He felt at one with all life forms, with the universe and all that was in it. Nothing was too dark and evil and out of tune with its true self to be embraced by that love and changed by its vibrancy.

His arms wanted to embrace, enclose relief from suffering. It was as though he could look through the solid, the dense and the heavy and see what was beautiful shining through a minute crack waiting to crack further and break free revealing the true radiance of what lay behind the covering.

13

Emma felt disappointment at having to leave the security of the Guardians, even though a protective body of men had been sent along to guide and lead them on their way. Kyoto was with her. He gravely walked alongside her interpreting her every wish and whim.

There was greyness about everything and eerie noises which were difficult to identify and locate. This frightened Emma. She heard a quiet internal voice speaking soft words of reassurance. "There is no need to be nervous. Take no notice of the noise around you. It is nothing. It is there to weaken your resolve. I repeat again, there is no need to be frightened and nervous. You are strong and capable. You have resources of courage that will stand you in good stead. You will come to no harm."

She found it hard to dissociate herself from what was going on around her. The extraneous noises impinged on her consciousness and made her start and jump in fright. There were ephemeral movements behind the branches of a tree. Eyes peered through the hedge, glittering and scintillating like diamonds in the reflective light. A figure popped up suddenly from the long grass and disappeared as suddenly as it had appeared.

Was she seeing things? Was it there or not there?

She rubbed her eyes as though that would help her to see more clearly. She tried to block out any outside noises so that she could interpret the noises she was listening for more clearly. She needed to interpret the sudden sound, the abrupt movement. She focussed her eyes in one direction where a new sound had originated and then another noise distracted her in another direction.

"Why are you so fearful?" said a quiet inner voice. "You are in a protective bubble shielded from all harm and hurt. Do you not trust me? Have we not walked safely together through many dangers?"

Then the Guardians, who had been their companions, indicated that they could go no further.

"You will not be alone," they added. "We will be near and will support you in times of difficulty. Our thoughts will be your thoughts. Be at peace. Physical distance will not separate us. Remember, you will never be alone. Feel safe in this knowledge."

The calmness and the peace which she had initially felt weakened and she felt fear surge inside her like an incoming tide. Kyoto and Emma were alone, deserted and unsupported.

Then she realised that they were indeed in a protective bubble. A massive, rainbow hued bubble that reflected all the colours of the prism. The bubble spun high into the air, high over the tallest branches of the trees. It floated upward, to where the clouds drifted in the sky. Rain spattered the outside of the bubble and the sun mirrored a rainbow of light from the droplets of water on its surface. It was held in the eye of the prism, multi-coloured, shiny and reflective.

The bubble rotated and spun.

It was like a soap bubble carried by the currents and movement of air. It reminded Emma of the happy hours she had spent watching the rainbow-hued bubbles riding up and up from the plastic wand which she had dipped into soapy water, and with a puff of her breath, magic moments occurred as the soapy spheres swung and danced and then splattered into droplets of moisture. She had idly watched the bubbles spiral upward, eddy in the wind, bobble away and then burst into nothingness, splatter into a fine spray of liquid.

What stopped the same thing happening to the bubble they were in? A touch, a puff of wind would make the insubstantial wall burst. There was no substance. It was like a protective womb primed to spawn its contents out.

Below the hills, valleys and rivers spread across the sorrel covered plains. Reflective light was everywhere. The snow had given way to the brightness of spring.

Kyoto broke the silence. "It is an illusion. What you see is not factual. Below you are savage wastes. Bitter cold and biting wind that freezes the flesh on your bones if the clothing you wear is not thermal and protective. This bubble is strong, though it may appear to be insubstantial. It is insulating us against the wintry conditions.

"Xylo's power is becoming stronger and stronger. Winter is taking over and the season is extending longer and longer through the year. There is a gradual cooling of the world's atmosphere. The change in the temperature means that a plaque of ice will extend wider and wider until it covers everything. This is the growth of Xylo's power. His magic is strong and he uses it with effectiveness. The power of good is being challenged by the powers of evil and darkness is extending its boundaries wider and wider."

"That cannot be," said Emma. "Bad can never overthrow good. Good will always rule supreme. You cannot believe the words that you speak. You are paying lip service to the darker side of your nature. I will not listen and be influenced by your words. They are untrue."

"It is your prerogative to believe it or not."

Emma felt a depressive gloom descend upon her. She felt difficulty in throwing off the pessimism of Kyoto's words. It was not like him. He was usually optimistic and encouraging, nothing seemed to get him down. Then the tenor of his speech changed.

"In the midst of this darkness and despair there is hope. There is a point on the earth's surface where the lines of energy run straight and true, and at that point it will join with the energy and the intuitivity of the moon to bring strength and power and goodwill. It will be a focal point for change. It will radiate out dispelling fear and darkness. Maximum energy will be brought to bear on this centre of renewal and rebirth. You are part of the God force and as such are a composite of the whole. All is possible. Have faith, believe in what you are and know that all will be well. Even as I speak, there are many motivated by an inner knowledge making their way on foot, directed by those inner forces of light. They are brave in the face of fear because they have that inner direction which is telling them what to do. At the same time, there is a supportive power upholding them with strength. I have been told to tell you this to give you courage and to make you aware that many are by your side. Many in this world love you and there are many in your world whose energy and love is upholding and renewing. Do not give in to despair and depression."

There was a reflective pause in the conversation.

"You have a task to carry through. You will have to walk in a physical sense alone, but do not fear that solitude because there are many near to comfort and uphold you. This mission will succeed, of that I am sure and it will bring peace and happiness. Love will motivate what happens and there will be a new balance and a change in the existing patterns as we know them in the world and universe at large."

"How do you know that this is about to happen? And what motivates this exodus at this point of time and the knowledge of where to go?"

"You do not understand the power of thought. Telepathic exchange has been forced upon us and has become like a second skin and is as natural as speech is to you. It is a swift method of communication and distance is no bar to its effectiveness. We are open to each other and no thought or action can be concealed or hidden. There are many in the universe who need signs or omens. They cannot believe the strength of that still inner voice and need constant reassurance from an outer level."

"All this is awakening some inner knowledge that I have always known, some distant memory, past conversations," said Emma sucking in her under lip thoughtfully and trying to remember what thought patterns were being jolted into consciousness. It was fragmented, distorted but Emma knew with a great sense of inner peace that she held this truth within her like a beacon of light. It was written in her life plan and in no way could she avoid or turn her back on it. It would always come around again, as if on a carousel, for her to face and deal with.

"There is a ring of stones on the Plain of Sol. It is there where the natural energies of the earth converge and come to a point on the surface. It is a fit place for the manifestation of light to take place."

Fragmented thoughts jolted into her consciousness like the pieces of a jigsaw puzzle waiting to be put together. Emma tried to make sense of them.

"You know there is a prophecy that I will be instrumental in these changes that you talk about. Scan quoted a verse about what we are discussing. At that time it did not make any sense but now with the words that you have spoken, I see a pattern emerging. Scan's words had more meaning than I realised at the time."

"All things are alive and vibrate at different frequencies. Earth, stones have a power of their own. Crystals and gem stones carry a healing strength within them."

"What has that to do with our mission?" said Emma in a mystified manner.

"All things radiate energy and have a different molecular structure. And they all have a part to play in what is about to happen."

"We are wasting time," said Emma.

"Be patient. All is well. There is time, plenty of time,

you will see. Things will happen in their due appointed time. Live each minute as it occurs and find that inner serenity and peace. Do not clutter your consciousness with inconsequentials. Keep it clear, like a still pool of water and allow it to develop its reflective, intuitive qualities. The guardians encourage the growth of good in the world. They will guide and protect."

As though in direct contradiction, a denial of these words, a giant pterodactyl creature appeared in the stormy, dark clouded sky and with a thrashing of mighty wings came straight towards the bubble with outstretched beak and sharp pointed tip built to perforate and split.

Fear buzzed like an angry bluebottle in Emma's ears. She closed her eyes and covered her ears with her hands. The bubble was about to burst. She had known all along that this was going to happen. It was inevitable, as inevitable as the bubbles she had blown as a child had disintegrated into a spray of moisture when they touched anything solid.

She looked through her fingers at the scene before her. There seemed no cover. The glass screen quality of the bubble left her exposed and open. Before her was a sight that made her cover her eyes in horror. The scaly pterodactyl bird had a following of small birds that darkened the sky with their movement. There were finch-like birds with grain eating beaks, and parrot type birds with multi-coloured feathers, Amazonian and bright. Small, wren birds, red-breasted robins and noisy starlings with their iridescent plumage reflecting in the light. The raucous cawing of large crows, the pied magpie and the wide span of the wings of the seagull thundered towards them aggressive and threatening.

They were milling around the bubble in a frenzied movement of wings. It was like a frieze of frenzy that seemed unending. Emma shuddered in fear. There was no way out of this. They could not possibly survive this onslaught. Through her fingers she could see the wide, gaping beaks shut against the casing of the bubble. She could see the pink insides of their mouths, the thin, needle pointed rows of teeth in the pterodactyl birds.

Then, as though aware of their lack of success because the bubble had held up against the onslaught, the hammering and pecking of beaks subsided. If Emma had not read somewhere that birdbrains were small and that most of their behaviour was instinctive rather than intelligent, she would have suspected they had withdrawn to confer about what action to take next.

The respite was a prelude to a further attack. She felt sure that they would not give up and accept defeat without further effort. Emma watched apprehensively. Nothing happened.

Emma felt warm and comfortable and the muscles of her eyelids kept involuntarily closing, and then she would abruptly jolt back into consciousness. Her eyelids felt too heavy to remain open. Then an exterior jolting movement made her open her eyes suddenly. The sight in front of her was unacceptable.

The birds, small and large, had marshalled like an army and were pushing, literally exerting mass movement on the bubble, movement that was pushing the bubble earthward to the jagged crags and the bottomless ravines that lay beneath in an endless mountainous, snow-capped range.

The birds were nose-diving the bubble earthward.

Kyoto's passive calmness abruptly changed to attentive watchfulness. He felt sure that the bubble was protected, that they could not come to harm, but the accelerated speed with which the bubble geared landward made him wonder whether his faith was justified. They were nearer and nearer the rugged, razor lacerating range of hills. The menacing up growth of jagged, granite, knife-edged rocks came closer and closer.

Kyoto's upstart of apprehension rebirthed Emma's fears. Anxiety gave way to open panic as the earth spiralled up to meet them. They were in line with the glitter of reflective light from what looked like a sheet of water cradled in the middle of the mountainous terrain. The closer they came, the more able they were to identify that the flashes of light came from a lake set high among the mountain peaks. The water below them came closer and closer. It was as though they were homing in on a beacon.

What was about to happen Emma wondered? The noise of her pulse echoed in her ears in a rapid, thudding beat. She was tense and rigid with fear. Then there was the impact of bubble on water and Emma thought 'This is the end' as the judder of impact jarred her spine and threw her head backward, whip lashed it out of control. She tried to grip on to something with fevered, outstretched fingers that found no substance on which to latch.

She was thrown across the diameter of the bubble. Her body rebounded from the opposite wall with meteoric force and then shunted to and fro as the bubble lost momentum and tried to regain stability and balance. The jolt of impact lessened and Emma saw in front of her a multi-dimensional picture. The flash of fishes among the weeds, the malachite sea green of her surroundings, a reflective movement, which shimmered with cool green light, the flicker of light and shade.

Seaweed floated in the water. The hair like fronds streaming sideward and, as a current of movement touched them; the fronds sailed upward and upward and then fell into an angled position. A jellyfish sailed idly by. An octopus, tentacles streaming behind made for the shelter of a large rock. A cold-eyed cod finned its way around the bubble curiously nosing toward the spherical shape, assessing the object before it with interest. A flat fish edged its way deeply into the sand at the bottom of the water until it was scarcely visible.

The cod's interest reactivated and it nosed the wall of the bubble expecting it to burst or to break into smaller bubbles and make for the surface. The sphere rolled like a ball along the bottom of the lake, jolted against a stony outcrop and plummeted down a precipitous ledge. It sank downward and downward, around and around, as it spiralled down a gully on the uneven bed of the lake.

Emma felt dizzy. Kyoto was unresponsive, totally immersed in what was happening to him, rolling around without control to the movement of the bubble. Emma wished she could get to him but she also had no control over what was happening.

The greenness and light had gone. There was murky darkness around them and no longer could Emma see Kyoto, or see through the wall of the bubble. It felt claustrophobic and shut in. This was the end. They would never get out of this situation. She was a prisoner as surely if she had been in a prison cell, a captive in a capsule under the sea. Who would look for them here? The blackness and darkness, as black as a raven's wing made her feel that she had to get out at all costs. Everything was pressing down upon her. She shrieked and thudded against the inner wall of the bubble.

Her breathing was becoming distressed. There did not seem to be enough air and she gasped and gulped in an effort to alleviate the situation. Sweat ran down her face and pooled under her fringe. Was this where her life was going to end, in among the mud and reeds at the bottom of a lake? They'd all be expecting her to return home. That thought would always be in the minds of the people she had left. They would hold on to that hope because nobody would find her body, not here at the bottom of a lake in some faraway country, and they would always be hoping that one day she would return. But she wasn't going to return, how could she there was no chance that she would be rescued.

There was an abrupt, cracking, rending noise and the bubble had split. It was breaking up under the pressure of the water. There was a rush of seawater into the exposed shell like an egg extruding its contents when cracked. They were bound to be thrown out, but the water lifted Emma and she felt herself rising and rising as though propelled from a cannon. She no longer had any breath left. Her head felt as though it was going to burst and she had a vague, distant, dreamy kind of feeling.

The half of the bubble in which Kyoto had been, shot like a bullet from a gun as though propelled by atomic power and broke the surface in a swell and upheaval of water. Kyoto was none the worse for the experience. He frantically tried to make out where he was. As the water settled he could see for a short distance but there was no evidence of what he was looking for. Fate could not be so cruel, not after all the difficulties they had weathered together. Emma was bound to be safe, she could not have drowned, and she must be all right. He could not believe that anything could have happened to her.

Not a ripple disturbed the still, calm water. Kyoto felt defeated. His belief that they had been protected had been strong. Now his expectations were dashed and he felt let down. He felt depressed and miserable.

Thunder crashed overhead and heavy clouds lowered over the surface of the water. It had become darker and he could hardly pick out anything even though he strained his eyes with effort. A flash of lightning lit up the darkened surface of the water with a bright clarity. It was too quick and unexpected for Kyoto to check where he was and whether there was anybody else near him on the lake. For a moment it was as bright as daylight and he had thought that he had seen something. He waited expectantly for another flash of lightning. He was sure there had been something out on the wind-ruffled water. A storm was lashing the water into white-topped waves. It was getting rougher and rougher and the wind blustered against his face and the water hit his face with such force that it felt as though a handful of gravel had been thrown at him.

He waited patiently, but no further lightning lit up the scene, thunder rumbled in the distance and there was an occasional flash on the horizon. The storm seemed to have moved away. Kyoto watched tense and anxious, straining his eyes into the darkness. He had been sure there had been something out there - a shape in the darkness, and movement bouncing on the disturbed surface of the lake.

He paddled the spherical shell in the direction that he had been looking, using his hands as oars to propel the shell along. He willed the thing to move swiftly and surely, as though it was a living thing with motivation of its own and it shot like an arrow from a bow. Kyoto tried to mentally talk to Emma. He thought of her bright, intelligent face.

"If you are out there, call and let me know that you are all right!" The only sound in reply was the movement of water against the shell.

14

Scan had a sense of accomplishment, completion. His meeting with the meditators had brought a deep sense of inner peace, like a still unruffled pool, with unplumbed depths. He wanted to stay in this oasis of peace, to remain with these people, to live in this happy state of unity and closeness.

"It is not for you, yet. It is a foretaste of what life could be. Take the memory of it back to your people and ponder on this wonder that has been shown to you. You have something precious that has been activated within you and this awareness will always remain with you. You have been charged with a new energy and this will help you to accomplish the task that is before you. This must be. A time will come when this duality between good and evil will become a thing of the past. All things are given the chance to grow, to change; nothing is static. Carry this peace that you have known to your people. There is good in all men. Reflect on this and know that to condemn another is to condemn yourself."

He was still and quiet for a short space of time. "I would thank you for the new knowledge that you have afforded us. You have aided us with new scientific facts about your body and the way it works, the cells and the hormones that circulate through the tissues. This may well be of use to us in the future. The panes of glass are like electrical scanners. They have recorded back to us the way your body works in health. Our cameras have taken sectionalised films and these will be of use to us when our services are needed in the years ahead. Your bodies are complex. Your thought processes are devious, and there are more in the universe who have minds that change direction and sequence like the frenzied movements of the mayfly. They hover and dart from one thing to another. "We are intuitive," said Scan.

"Not intuitive enough to know that good is supreme. You still fear and do not believe in the power and strength that you have within you. You anticipate evil and trouble. And therein lies your difficulty - the lack of belief in the good within you. This body that you have is but an overcoat which houses the real you, struggling to express itself in the world in which you live."

Scan answered. "If you lived in our world you would realise the fear of living under the power of darkness. Our world is struggling with the power of evil."

"This need not be so. Your despair, anger and resentment feed and grow upon themselves, as do all negative thoughts. They accumulate like a fog, obscuring you from the light to which you really are part of, to which you belong. It creates wars, disease and unhappiness. This is necessary at this time for your growth but it will not always be so. You will eventually be joyful peoples, who live in peace and an awareness of where they belong and who they are."

Scan felt a surge of energy that flooded him with hope and contentment.

"Go into the abyss in peace. You will forget our existence, as the world is not yet right for us to show ourselves. The way before you is clear. Follow it with ease and be of good heart. The marks of your footsteps are clear upon the plan of the universe. Go in peace."

Scan made his way back to his followers with the strength of certainty in his bones. There was a dignity about his bearing that was felt by the men who apprehensively awaited his return. They looked at his face with an awesome respect and were glad this man had been chosen as their leader by the dominant majority

"You look as though what you have hoped for has come about," said one man, questioningly assessing the peaceful look on Scan's face. "That all will be well and our quest will succeed despite the dangers we have met and you carry with you an assurance that we are on the right path."

"There are many paths and they all take you in the same direction. Do not fear all will be well. Follow your heart," said Scan in reply.

"There was a rumbling noise shortly before your return which made us fearful for our safety."

"We thought it could have been a rock fall which could block the way before us."

"Do not fear, your life plan is already mapped out. Live in the day and deal with what is there before you to the best of your ability, that is all that is asked of you, nothing else, just to be."

Scan was aware in some strange way of what was about to happen in the future. He could see the life plan ahead in time for the men he was speaking to. This was something new to him and it hung heavily on his shoulders. He could see the one man returning to the orange groves where he belonged, being greeted by his young wife with great love and tenderness, and another picture flashed into his mind of them together with a young baby in the mother's arms and the pride and happiness on their features as they looked into the baby's face with great joy at this perfect miniature being which they had produced. They marvelled at the perfection of the tiny fingers and toes and their happiness was plain for all to see.

Another man joined the conversation expressing his loyalty to Scan and his hope that not so very far from now they would be united with their families. Scan saw that this would never happen. He saw sadness, sorrowing and mourning for this good man and a wife who would take many years before she could get over her loss. This ability to see into the heart of things frightened Scan. He was not sure what was happening. He did not want the responsibility of knowing these things. It sat heavily upon his mind. People often wanted to know the future and whether it held good news for them, but the future could give evidence which was best left unsaid and nothing would be gained by revealing what he knew was about to happen. He sensed he had to discriminate about what words he said and what he left unsaid, and in his silence lay a deep, poignant loneliness.

He did not want to know when and how he would leave the world and move into a new dimension of understanding. It took time for him to realise that he had not received the gift to look into his own future. It was a closed book and for this he was glad. He was learning to trust and live each day as it came and deal with each situation as it came into his life.

What practical use could he make of this gift? It seemed to him that it created a divide and cut him off from his fellow men, but it was there within his life so he had to accept and see where it led him in the future.

A rumble echoed through the cavernous passages.

"There it is again."

"Could it be Xylo exerting his power because he knows where we are and is trying to put obstacles in our pathway?"

"That may be true," said Scan thoughtfully. "But I am more inclined to think that is a natural phenomenon. This area has had the odd earthquake or so."

The low rumble and the sound of falling debris echoed once again through the underground passages.

"Come we are wasting time," said Scan.

They followed his lithe, slim body as he went ahead through the gloom. There was dust in the atmosphere and this made them cough and splutter.

"You know," said one of the men, "there's a glow

about him, like a firefly which helps us to follow in his footsteps. It's almost uncanny."

The rumbling grew in intensity and clouds of dust and fragments of stone fell across the path in front of them. It got in their eyes and made them cough.

"I told you so. There's more afoot here than bears to be thought of. There is some power that is trying to block our progress."

"Just a belly ache," said another of the men optimistically. "Nowt to worry about."

"Mark my words, we'll be lucky if we get out of here alive. It'll be our end."

As though in response to the foreboding words, the rumbling increased in intensity and a column of stone fell across the way dividing the group into two parties.

"There's no way through this," said one voice.

"There's nothing we can do but go back the way that we have come."

To add to the confusion, the fall seemed to have activated some animal that must have lived in the deep, underground caverns. A low growl grew in intensity. It sounded menacing and aggressive and the men wondered what it was that had been disturbed by the fall. How close was it? They had no weapons to ward off an attack.

The noise seemed to grow in intensity and pitch. Ahead their way was blocked. Behind was a predator, fearful because of the sudden caving in of the passage and ready to attack. It bayed like a hound tracking down its prey and the darkness made its location impossible to gauge. It could be coming towards them or it could be a distance away and no threat to them. What should they do? They had to turn and face their attacker.

"You!" indicated a man who took charge of the situation. "Push that overhanging rock."

"That I'll not do," said the man in a frightened way. "It'll cause another fall to occur."

"That's what I want."

"Are you mad? We'll be cut off. Walled in an airless pocket."

"Do as I say. There is no time to lose. A partial blockage will act as a defence, a barrier to what is out there." He turned to another man. "You collect stones. Select ones that are not too big and that you can throw at whatever is coming towards us. It might frighten it off. And heap them up so that we have them at hand ready to use."

The noise seemed to be coming closer and closer. The howling echoed threateningly through to where they were and some stones started to fall as though activated by the movement. They resolutely pushed at the overhang and felt the stones moving under their fingers. There was a deafening noise and acrid dust rose up from the mound of rock in front of them. They could still see over the top of the stones, once the dust had settled, along the uneven floor of the underground tunnel.

There was silence once the noise and the dust had settled broken by a frightened yelp of pain, as though a dog had been hit by a car and was injured.

"Listen," said one of the men.

The yelping went on and on.

"It sounds as though the animal is trapped."

"Whatever it is, if that's the case, at least we are safe. Let's put all our energies into getting back to the rest of the party."

"You can't mean to tell me that you'd leave an injured animal trapped without any hope of it getting free?" He hesitated for a moment. "Well, I can't do that. I have to see what I can do to help it."

"There's something wrong with you. If you succeed in what you are about to do, what do you think it'll do? Thank you? No such thing. It'll probably tear you apart for your pains."

"How would you like to be left to a lingering death underground?"

116

"You have too much sympathy and compassion. One of these days it will lead you into trouble."

"What you say will not make me change my mind. I'm going to see if I can be of any help."

The howling and the piteous yelping punctuated the words of the conversation with unfailing regularity.

"It's a trap. Perhaps it's a deliberate attempt to intimidate us. It may be waiting there."

"To do what? You have too much imagination. You credit it with more intelligence than it probably has. You stay here and try and contact the rest of the group who have got cut off on the other side of the fall. Let them know that we are alive otherwise they may go on ahead of us."

He turned and clambered over the barrier of stone that rattled down like scree beneath his feet. He jumped down and made his way along the underground tunnel in the direction from where the sound was centred. He couldn't help feeling an element of fear gnawing away inside him. Had he been unwise to take this action?

There had been another fall of stones and this was where he found the creature. It was partially crushed by a large flat slab of rock. It drew back in fear and terror from the approaching figure and growled menacingly, deep in its throat. It was a slimy, subterranean creature with warty encrustations over its body. Was this the creature that a short while ago had held them in abject terror, a brave band of men who outnumbered it many times?

It cringed back and piteously yelped in a threatened, frightened way. If only all their fears turned out to be small and no cause for alarm. The man spoke quietly and persuasively to the creature. It did not look gravely injured. If he put his hand under the overhang perhaps it could ease itself free. The problem was that any sudden movement could cause another landslide and that could endanger both their lives.

It quietened under his gentle, unprovocative approach

117

and made no noise. It followed the man's movements with round, nocturnal eyes, the corners of which, every so often, hooded like the eyes of an unwell cat. It should have had fur, not warty outgrowths of skin. Its eyes were childlike and appealing, like the round, wondering eyes of a few days old kitten

He held out the back of his hand in a gesture of friendship, so that the animal could sniff and recognise a friend, and then dared to touch the creature gently with his fingers. It drew back but did not make any attempt to bite or snarl.

"Let's see what we can do." The slab of stone was preventing the stones above from collapsing, but a slight shift would bring everything down. If the stone fell the creature would die, there was no doubt about that. Then the man noticed air fan across his face. He looked up reacting to the unexpected sensation. There was a pinpoint of light in the far distance.

Could the fall have revealed a parallel tunnel that ran alongside the path they had been following? Would this enormous piece of fortune provide a way out? If there was further rock fall it may block any chance they had of escape. He looked reflectively at the creature. He couldn't leave it here, somehow he had to gain its confidence so that it didn't react with fear and do the unexpected. There was the sound of movement coming towards them.

"Softly, softly," he said soothing the renewed yelping of the animal and the creature responded to the gentleness of his hands. The man waited apprehensively for what would appear from the opening that the fall had revealed. Tension registered on the muscles of his face. Then his face relaxed as he recognised the man in front of him. They embraced in a joyful, delighted fashion.

"Scan, I cannot believe it is you."

The creature growled in a menacing, threatening way.

"What have we here?" said Scan.

"Careful, it is easily frightened. If it struggled and moved suddenly it could cause the roof to collapse." He turned to the animal and in a soft tone of reassurance gently soothed and patted him. "Nobody's going to hurt you." The creature became passive again under the healing strength of the man's fingers and looked at them both with his large eyes. The man went on talking to Scan.

"Just as you came I felt air on my face and I was investigating the possibility of there being a way to the surface. Can't you feel the movement in the atmosphere? Every so often there is a draught as though a wind is blustering in from outside. There, feel it then? I felt it quite clearly on my cheek."

There was a break in his speech for a moment or so as their attention centred on what they had been talking about.

"You may well be right," said Scan thoughtfully. "A tunnel to the surface...!"

"If this fall had not happened we could have gone on and on, deeper and deeper underground. Steady! Steady! Scan will do you no harm. You'll be safe with him. He won't hurt you."

It seemed to recognise that there was no threat and lapsed into watchful silence.

"It doesn't look as though it is pinned down," said Scan thoughtfully. "There's room there for it to squeeze out, let me feel and check."

The animal growled low in its throat in a warning way but responded to the friendship Scan showed as he allowed the animal to sniff at his hand and get used to this new smell and recognise it was not an enemy and meant him no harm.

"It seems almost too frightened to move. I think it must have damaged itself in some way and movement is painful."

The creature was moving its head up and down and its nostrils were sniffing this new scent in an investigative way. Seeming satisfied, he rested his head upon an overhanging rock and watched them.

"Tell you what, let's take a few steps away from him as though we mean to leave and see what he does."

They edged further along the passageway. Ahead of them they could see the pinpoint of light and they felt the air cool on their faces. The eyes of the creature followed them in a quiet, docile manner. They heard his yelp as they disappeared from view. They moved back a few steps and watched it struggling to break free, eager to follow them, but from where they were it looked as though its leg was damaged. It had wriggled out from under the slab of stone and was coming towards them dragging its rear leg. But it was gaining ground and moved towards them purposefully, its tail-less rear end moving backward and forward with pleasure, greeting them like old friends and it rolled submissively over on to its back, exposing his stomach to them as though saying 'You are in charge'. Scan rubbed its chest and it showed pleasure, and touched Scan on the arm with its paw as though asking for more.

"Good boy! I'll fix that leg," Scan said. "I'll see to it while you go back and get the others. We need to move on. The light that is there at the end of the tunnel shows that there is still time for us to get on with our quest. Xylo has not taken total control of the universe. There is still time to change events. Total darkness is his dominion. A starless, moonless darkness that engulfs everything throughout the time span. The world as we know it will die. No seeds will germinate and life will be extinguished." He paused momentarily. "Perhaps, one day a new life form will mutate from the basic cells which survived from the present time but it will not bear much resemblance to what we know as life at the present time. If Xylo is dominant, all oxygen dependant species will be bred out. The landscape will be bare and barren. There will be dust bowls and deserts where once there were green fields and woods and rivers that ran clear and deep where fish used to dart in among the reeds. Our civilisation will only be found aeons later, during archaeological digs and from surviving history books. But less of this, the power of evil has not yet got full control and may never do so if we carry through what we are meant to accomplish. Good will rule supreme and there will be harmony and balance again, peace where there is fear."

He deftly bandaged the leg of the unprotesting creature.

"He seems to have taken to us. You laugh! What is tickling your fancy?"

"It's nothing. Just a memory brought back by the way we reacted when we heard the howling and yelping that this poor thing made. It sounded so ferocious, we thought it must be at least bear size and bound to be aggressive and on the attack. Just shows, we are too much on the defensive, expect the worst when there may be no threat. You're no threat to man nor beast, are you boy?" he said patting the animal on the head. "It's all in the mind, this fear of the unknown, fear of what we do not understand. Let me tell you of what happened one day. There was a story in the local press about the escape of a wild animal from a passing circus and one particular night we were awoken by a loud noise in the garden. It was around the side of the house, so we crept out with sticks in our hands to defend ourselves. 'You stand back', said someone. 'Do not get too close. It may get frightened if cornered, and attack'. There we were, this attack thing that always features so prominently in our reactive behaviour. It sounded like a large creature, very large.

"'Yes,' said I. 'You could hear it upstairs in the bedroom. It woke me up. What do you think it could be? Perhaps it's that animal which was reported in the press to have escaped and people were advised not to approach it'.

"But there was nothing around the side of the house. Certainly no large, wild animal but on closer inspection there were two hedgehogs indulging in sexual activity, snuffling and snorting at the foot of the hedge."

He laughed at the memory that had flooded back into his mind. "That taught me a lesson. Things are not always what they seem."

15

"Is that you Kyoto?" said a disembodied voice from the murky, misty darkness "Kyoto! Kyoto!" it entreated, "please answer me." There was silence for a short space of time and then the voice continued, "I know that you are there, but I cannot see you. This is no time for games. I am frightened. The mist is so dense that I cannot see a thing." There was a further silence broken only by the hiss of the wind on the water. " Kyoto, Kyoto."

Kyoto heard the voice and edged the half spherical shell in the direction from which he had sensed contact. There was increased hope in his heart. Emma was alive. She had survived the nosedive into the lake. They had both come through this new ordeal. They were survivors.

"Here I am, Emma. I'll soon be with you."

Then he saw the dark shape of an object on the water in front of him and the white blur of a face peering intently through the mist which wuthered, thickened and thinned in density according to the movement of the wind. One minute he could see her and the next minute she was obscured from sight.

Then they were together again. She was leaning over to him totally oblivious to the balance of the object she was floating in, reaching out with outstretched arms to him.

"Be careful or you'll overbalance and you'll be in the water. Keep still," but Emma was already clambering undauntingly across to him.

"I am so relieved to see you," she said. "It was horrid, alone in the dark mist. We seem to have landed high in the mountains, and the thrust of the landing drove us deep down into a lake, set high among the hills and I could not believe what was in front of me - numerous sea creatures, plants and fish. As the sphere hit the water and nose-dived under the surface it was like being under the sea or looking through a glass bottomed boat at the colourful shoals of fish darting among the weed and sea grass. Here an octopus floated past, tentacles trailing behind it like the hair of a mermaid. And a jellyfish as translucent as glass floated under them.

"To all appearances we landed in clear water set high in the hills. I thought it was all an illusion and we'd been misled into thinking we were over a barren range of hills and we'd really been over a wide expanse of deep-sea water. It is incredible! There must be some explanation, some geographical fault, and a rift in the rock formation from the coast running deep inland under the surface strata. It could be a blowhole connection between the hills and the coast.

"Strange that the sea water can rise to such a height. There must be a form of siphonic, osmotic effect. If I hadn't seen what I've seen, I'd think it was a make believe story or a fantasy."

As she spoke, a porpoise somersaulted up into the air alongside them and fell back into the water with a swell of movement. It nosed around in the water near them making tuneful noises of companionship.

"Did you see that? That certainly wasn't a figment of the imagination. That's added proof of our experience. The two of us were together when we saw it this time. It was not a mirage or a visual distortion." She laughed in a way which spoke of seeing the incredible, the mystical. She knew how a visionary feels when an attempt to put into words what has been experienced falls flat and lacks the true essence and meaning and everybody wonders what all the excitement is about.

"A porpoise up in the mountains." She giggled in a

mischievous manner. "All this up on a mountain top." She giggled again in sheer disbelief. "This would cause a sensation in our land and attract thousands of sightseers. It was the same when corn circles appeared overnight near where we live. People came in their hundreds to look at them first hand. There'd be thousands of people prepared to go to any end to see porpoises and dolphins in the hills. There'd be snorkelling and deep sea diving in no time and making a commercial proposition out of it. There'd be imported sand to create beach conditions and a miniature railway run to make easy access so that thousands of people could experience at first hand this new-found novelty."

There was silence for a brief time then Emma said, "Do you think the lake is tidal?" And as an afterthought, "Could we pass through the subterranean passage to the coast?"

"It's possible," said Kyoto. "But I've never heard of anything like this before. If that is so, there must be a tidal time involvement. High and low tides. There is a possibility that anybody going through could choose the wrong time and get caught in the tunnel as the tide changes."

"And drowned," completed Emma, but she thrust away the thought and laughed. "Fish in the mountains, a shoal of mackerel, and a blue-toothed shark on the highest peak. At least you don't have to wait for the trawler to come in. Fresh hake for supper, herring and haddock for breakfast."

Their attention was drawn back to the dark, still waters enshrouded with mist. A blood-curdling, bellowing noise reverberated through the hills, echoing from crag to crag with the impact of thunder, startling in its abruptness.

"What was that?" said Emma in a hushed voice. "What could it be?"

"To the shore," said Kyoto. "Paddle towards the land. That is our only hope of safety."

"But...." started Emma.

"Listen to what I say. When I say one, two, three, start paddling with your hands. We have to synchronise. Listen to what I say. One, two, three."

The bellowing noise was becoming louder and louder. They were moving quite fast now over the surface of the water. Emma could see what looked like a long neck extending ten to twelve feet above the water.

"It's an animal. It's gaining on us. Whatever will we do?"

"Don't look back," warned Kyoto. "Concentrate on what you are doing. There's rhythm to our stroke. Lose synchronisation and we'll slow down and the thing will gain on us."

"It is getting closer and closer," said Emma in a quivery voice.

"Keep your eyes to the front. Do as I say," said Kyoto urgently.

"I've got to look back," said Emma. "It is closer to me than it is to you. I've got to know where it is. I can't stand being chased. I'm frightened that it will gain ground and suddenly lunge out and grab me."

"Don't look back. Do as I say."

The momentum of the shell was moving them across the water swiftly, and the distance between them and the creature was widening. Emma took this in with one quick glance over her shoulder, but this glance cost her dearly. Rhythm was lost and their speed slackened.

"One, two, three," said Kyoto trying to gain their lost momentum. It didn't work, their speed slowed still further and spun to a standstill.

"There's nothing for it, we'll have to swim." He looked in the direction in which he thought there was land.

Kyoto gave Emma a push. Her body hit the water with a splash. She went under and then came to the surface spluttering with anger and irritation. There was nothing for it. She'd have to follow. Kyoto was already fifty yards ahead of her. She could see his head bobbing around in the water. She couldn't believe that he would do that, leave her on her own.

She could see the long neck of the sea creature getting closer and closer and see the way his mouth was drawn back in a snarl, ready to bite and lacerate with those sharp teeth. She felt as though paralysed into inaction, her arms and legs refused to move. She felt caught in some dream when she was the victim being chased and was frozen to the spot unable to get a muscle to work for her.

Just as she had decided that there was nothing that she could do, and she had closed her eyes to obscure the sight of the terrifying creature that every second was getting closer and closer, she felt that she was moving. Not moving in a physical sense but being carried along involuntarily. She had no say in the matter. She was caught in a fast moving current and she realised that the distance between her and the long-necked creature was widening. It was a speck on the horizon, getting smaller and smaller, until she could no longer pick it out in the distance. The bellowing noise had receded and she could no longer hear it.

The movement of the water was becoming swifter and swifter and the velocity was drawing her under the surface. She struggled, but any physical protest was useless. The water was being siphoned as though through a gigantic straw. There was a seething, sucking sound which was getting louder and louder. Emma tried to yell but choked on the water that ran into her mouth. She was lost in an avalanche of peaked sound that thundered and foamed around her. She was thrust and belched forward without volition.

Her hands clasped on to something solid and she clung desperately on to the moving object, which seemed to be coasting through the water with purpose. Emma, while being in shock, realised that the thing was alive. She felt the ripple of muscle in movement, the tension and relaxation of the body. It made an animal singing noise that was gentle, reassuring and comforting. She felt things were becoming hazy and distant as though she was losing consciousness and desperate for air. She could remember thinking 'Is this what it is to drown?' She felt distanced from what was happening to her body, as though it wasn't really happening. She was drifting away. It wasn't an unpleasant sensation, merely a dimming of physical awareness. There was a light and a feeling of peace, of drifting, drifting as though on clouds soft as down.

And just as there seemed to be no recollection, just a sensation of being carried, floating in a serene state of peacefulness, not really concerned about what was happening, she was thrust on to the surface of the water gasping and gulping for breath. Her breathing was harsh and rasping as she coughed and tried to get her breath. Above her she saw the dark sky. Then she was drawn back under the water and once again her senses were becoming dim and distant.

Her struggle was lessening. She felt pleasantly distant and vague. Nothing really mattered, not now. There was singing and explosive patterns of light spiralled and flickered in her head. Nothing mattered any more - nothing at all.

16

David was dragged along the passageway. His body felt keelhauled, lacerated and abraded by the roughness of rock and sand. He was thrust into a room where the brightness of the light temporarily blinded his vision, and thrown to the floor in front of a raised dais, enshrouded in darkness, engulfed in blackness.

"You dare to challenge the power of Xylo," said twittering voices in a chorus. "Your flesh is weak, prey to human ills. If we dig our claws into it, does it not bleed? If we scratch it, does it not mark?"

Six black cats sat in a row, sable as darkness, their fur reflecting the jet of night

"Miaow!"

A raised line came up on David's skin where the claws had been drawn down his leg. He covered it with his hand.

"See, he feels pain. Does it hurt? If you do as we say you have nothing to fear. Xylo has given us power. The power to inflict punishment, if what we command is not obeyed. You will learn that, if you defy us in any way. Miaow!!" They looked at David in a penetrating, in-depth manner.

"We do not feel pain so it is difficult to know how much pain we inflict. It can sometimes be fatal." They cackled in a harsh, abrasive way.

The nine pterodactyls, bat like creatures flapped their wings in a demanding, attentive way and squawked aggressively.

"You also have powers. Miaow!" said the black cats to

the noisy, attention seeking bats. "Xylo has instructed us to sit at the gate and make anyone entering the kingdom worthy of being in our presence. We purify them of their good, of all individuality, of everything that they have been trained to accept as right. You do well to fear. Dread is building up inside you. Fear is eating at your entrails. You will know fear, such fear as you have never experienced. We have you indexed, pigeon-holed and we can manipulate your shell." A shriek of inane laughter greeted the words. "You are fearful. Your legs are turning to jelly. That is good. You are on the way to growth, to being tamed, to being the loyal servant of Xylo." They seemed to swell in size and importance in a visible way. "Xylo is all powerful. Look into our eyes, empty your shell, let the husk only remain, trickle all the mannerisms, the ideas, the thoughts, hopes, all that makes you David into this bowl."

In front of the purring cats was an enamelled container patterned with strange, moving shapes, from which incense laden smoke rose upward in a spiral. David knew that he had to look away. Away from the empty, cavernous eyes which seemed to be absorbing him out of himself.

"You dare to challenge the supremacy of Xylo?"

David dared not look upward. He felt the person that he accepted as himself being absorbed slowly into disintegration. He struggled to resist the spell. It was compulsive, hypnotic. It was not an unpleasant sensation, vague, drifting, but he knew instinctively that it would be the end of life as he had known it, if he succumbed to the indoctrination. David was aware of what was happening, what it was all about.

"You will be punished for this insolence. You will learn it is not wise to rebel and show disobedience to the power of Xylo."

He was dragged into an enclosed cell carved into the rock and the only light was blocked with a large boulder that was rolled into the opening, trapping him in a tomb of black, impenetrable darkness. The last words he heard from his torturers rang in his ears.

"Reflect on your behaviour, what you have done and what is going to happen to you if you disobey and pit your wits against the magnificence, the might, the power of Xylo." Time seemed endless. There was no sign of life. Silence, which seemed to stretch into an endless void, tomblike darkness that seemed impenetrable, surrounded him. He felt that he was spinning like a top, going faster and faster in its circle of orbit and then as swiftly decelerating to a standstill so that he was dizzy and off balance, even though he was seated on the floor. Half of him wondered if there was a floor. Was he suspended in an unbounded area of space, stretching into eternity, without beginning or end?

He did not know where he was or what was happening. He was shut in on himself, and a dreamlike detachment made him part of scenes where the past figured with dramatic intensity.

"Mother, is that you? You know the day when we had decorations up for the party? It was snowing. I had my nose up against the windowpane watching the snowflakes drifting to a point in front of my eyes. You said I have something to tell you. You were wearing the same dress today as you wore that day - lace at the neck, tight waisted and full-skirted. You were pretty, so pretty that I had to look again and again to fill myself with the sight of your prettiness. 'What is it Mum?' 'It's a surprise.' 'Tell me, Mum.' 'Well, it's like this,' you hesitated. A cascade of snow fell from the roof and past the window where you sat. I was snuggled close to you. 'I wish you'd get on with it. I'm dying of curiosity.'

"You smiled in a enigmatic, quizzical way and a dimple appeared on the left side of your cheek and your eyes narrowed and crinkled at the corners. 'You know your friend Danny? Not so long ago, he had a baby sister.' 'Yes, he did and it's a flaming nuisance, stops them from going out together or doing anything special. Always needs to be fed or changed.' He had held his nostrils together at the thought. 'Ugh! There's no time for anybody but the baby. It takes all their space and attention.' David remembered vividly the grim picture his friend had painted since the arrival of his new brother. 'Can't have his friends in because if you make a noise it will wake the baby and you ought to hear the racket when that happens. I feel sorry for my friend and I'm glad we haven't got a baby in the house.'

"You looked rather taken aback at this strong response to what you had said and went on 'There's a baby on the way for us too.' 'A baby! You can't be serious. You must be joking.' I had stared at you in disbelief. The noise of someone filling the coal hod had broken the silence. 'Have you told Emma?' 'She's really pleased. Is looking forward to pushing the pram down the road and showing off the new arrival.' 'She would,' he had said, in a disgruntled way."

Then the picture of his Grandmother came up on the screen and faded back.

"Mamma, Grandma," he said.

And then he was crying. "Dad, I didn't do it. Honest, I didn't. It's not true."

"I'll make you speak the truth if it's the last thing that I do," said his father in an authoritative tone. "Playing truant from school. If our neighbour hadn't seen you and got back to your mother we wouldn't have known."

"I hadn't done my homework and I was frightened of going in without it. You don't know what the teacher's like when he's in a temper."

"Stop snivelling boy and take your punishment like a man."

"No, Dad. Please, Dad. Don't do it. Please. I won't do it again. I promise."

A stream of light temporarily blinded him and he huddled away from the abrasiveness of it.

"Go away. I won't do it. Honest I won't."

They caught him by his arms and dragged him firmly outside and he screamed and yelled. "Don't do it. I'll promise I'll be good. I'll never do it again."

"That's what we want, my boy," said a soft, persuasive voice. "I think he's ready to give in," purred the black cat. "Listen to what we say."

He felt something being drawn out of his body as though on extended threads.

"I am David, David," he moaned. "David."

"Put him in the lobster pot," said the voice in a harsh, irritated way. "There's no point in wasting any further time on him. He's not ready."

He was shackled firmly around the neck and the ankles to a pole that ran through the middle of a wicker basket construction that he felt jolt from its stationary position.

"I'll do as you say," cried David.

"You will that. They all do," said a background voice and the wicker framework continued to jolt downward into the dark.

"Let me out. Let me out," he yelled but the only answer was the sound of his own voice echoing back in his ears.

There was a splash of water and a sudden jolt as the wicker basket hit the surface. The water began to rise on the inside of the basket as it sunk slowly down and down. How far would it go? thought David. Did they intend to drown him? It was up to his upper thigh now. Icy fingers gripping his limbs, making them lose all sensation and feel heavy and numb. The icy coldness slowly moved upward to his stomach, diaphragm, neck. At this point David struggled to free himself, feeling the coldness of the water lapping at his chin. Terror welled up in him as it grew closer and closer to his mouth and nose but his struggles worsened the situation. The level stopped and rose in waves, so that it ran into his mouth and he swallowed the bad tasting liquid and spluttered and choked. A steady, calm voice cajoled him into staying still.

"Don't fight it. Keep as still as you can."

"I'm going to drown, drown." His panic argued with the internal voice that patiently repeated his injunction. "Keep your head. Don't panic."

"I'm going to drown."

Then David realised that the wicker basket had jolted to a standstill. There was no further movement. He waited apprehensively for a sign that it had dislodged itself and was moving again, but the basket remained where it was and there was the grind of machinery and the water level dropped to chest height as the basket moved upward. The noise of turning cranking movement stopped and there was silence.

David listened intently until he imagined that his ears were hurting with the intensity he applied to the situation. His eardrums throbbed and dizzy, light coloured sensations splattered on the darkness, like a film when the numbers are phasing out to the start but there was no start.

All that remained was this sensation of floating, of elevation, nothing solid underfoot and this psychedelic run through of faces and situations from the past.

"Mum, I'm frightened. Please don't leave me."

"You're a big boy now."

"Please stay with me. It's dark."

"Dark is all right. It's warm and comfortable."

"I'm scared. My teeth are chattering."

"I thought I heard something like pans clattering," said his mother. "So that's what it was?"

"Mum, it's not funny, really it isn't. I'm frightened. Talk to me. Don't make fun and joke."

"Everything's all right. I'm going downstairs."

"Talk to me. Don't go away."

"Lie down, everything will be all right. There's no need to be frightened of the dark. I'll leave this night light on and I'll only be in the other room. Call out if you want me."

She held his hand for a short time and then got up to

leave the room. "When I look in next time I bet you'll be fast asleep."

He watched her go with fear and apprehension.

"Don't leave me," he sobbed in a hysterical, frightened manner.

She was gone with a swish of skirts and a backward glance of reassurance. He drew back in terror. There was a tiger with large, yellow eyes in the corner by the wardrobe. And there by the curtain was a monkey doing somersaults over the curtain rail. And on the dressing table a bear with black, indelible fur. And hanging from the lamp flex that dangled down the wall was a large snake, with a long tongue flicking in and out, in and out.

He screamed in abject terror.

"Get me out!"

There was no answer to his terrified screams.

It was water trickling into his mouth and making him splutter and choke that made him come back abruptly from his disembodied, fantasy world in which he had been lost. He was shivering with cold, but even as he became aware of his surroundings he started to lose contact again and to subtly sink into the floating internal world that he had just left.

"That you David?"

"I'm here."

"David of the white rock." His voice joined the chorus of singers rousing the lilting cadences of the Welsh song.

"Flowers in the rock garden."

"Sand between the toes."

"David, David."

"Waves upon the beach."

"David."

"Mamma. Dadda."

He heard himself shrieking. "Don't touch me. Don't touch me. I'm only little."

David opened his eyes. There, before him, were the

three black cats and six pterodactyl bat like creatures.

"I am David," he mouthed in a thick, mucous tone and slumped to the floor.

"He's dead," cackled the three cats in unison. "Dead," and they laughed in an evil, menacing manner. "He's a shell."

Even then David managed to mouth, "I am David," and repeated "Daffydd y garreg wen, David of the white rock," in a dim hazy way remembering the song that he had sung in school, and because his name was David it had meant something special to him. "I am David, David of the White Rock."

17

The next thing Emma heard was the sound of a bird singing its heart out above her head. She opened her eyes and a brightly coloured bird flew from a tree down on to the dune grass. It was black and grey with patches of red, blue and yellow on its rump, head and wings. It was singing one note after the other, an endless trickle of quavering notes. Its repertoire seemed endless.

Emma turned from her back on to her stomach and watched the twitching movement of the black tail and the throbbing in the throat as the muscles moved in song. The sea stretched as far as the eye could see. A mirror-like placidity ruffled the shoreline as the waves gently broke and receded. The sand was warm under her body and she ran the grains through her open fingers, watching them fan outward as they fell to the beach. There were beaches in heaven she thought.

Idly she picked up a large conch shell and put it to her ear and listened to the murmur of soft sounds which whispered in a up and down swell like the movement of the ocean. She thought that people should be here to greet her - to make her welcome. She'd always thought that would happen in the other world. People that she had known and loved who would embrace her with affection. But nothing broke the emptiness of the scene before her that stretched towards a promontory of rock that reached out into the sea. At the foot of these rocks creamed white surf, like an irregular band of ribbon.

Emma lifted herself up supporting the upper part of her

body with her elbows. Not a movement fretted the silver stillness of what lay in front of her. But wait! What was that red object which was flapping irregularly in the movement of the wind? It looked like a scarf. Where had she seen it before? Where could it have been? She was sure it was something to do with Kyoto. Could Kyoto be in heaven with her?

The thought amused her. Heaven did not seem any different from earth. She pinched her arm. The flesh on her body was the same, solid and firm. Had time changed?

Puzzled, Emma looked around her. A feeling of discomfort surged up inside her. Was heaven being alone? Then her mind made a definite association. She had seen that piece of red cloth before. She knew that it belonged to Kyoto. Where could he be?

Emma took a deep breath. "Kyoto! Can you hear me? Kyoto!" Her voice got thinner as it echoed around the bay from cove to headland, from headland to beach. There was no sign of life, other than the mewing sound of the birds. There was emptiness and space, and the breaking of the surf on the beach.

18

Kyoto found it not so difficult to tolerate the underwater movement. He had a better lung capacity than Emma and he did not lose his consciousness to the same extent. The underground passage was long and curving and the pull of the current was strong. Kyoto realised that they had been drawn into the connecting rift that led from the mountain lake to the sea.

At low tide all the water was drawn, sucked back into the salt ocean taking much of the marine life with it. Perhaps that accounted for the health of the sea life and the way they thrived away from their natural habitat, though there must be a residue left in the muddy water at the bottom of the lake. The downward tidal surge was powerful like a tidal race, or like a typhoon spiral going deep down to the bed of the ocean. The water surged through the cavernous opening.

Kyoto was swept along like a piece of driftwood, grazed against rocks in among the tidal debris, drawn into the race. Then he was out in the open again being drawn into a spiral, sucked around and around, down and down in a circular fashion that made him dizzy and disorientated. Was there a bottom? Would he ever reach the end of this spiral and come back up to the surface on a parallel one? Would he survive being under water for such a length of time? Even now he felt distant, with a pressure on his chest, as though his consciousness was losing awareness. He felt far away, as though falling into a deep sleep.

Then, as a mere thread of consciousness remained, he

was ejected like vomit out of the spiral on to the wet sand. It was solid beneath him but water was beginning to wash around his body, lifting it up and then setting him down on the sand again. Distantly he heard the thunder of surf, and the rattle of pebbles being drawn in the undertow and the noise as the water ran from between the stones and they lifted and fell in a rhythmic movement. It was like a song in his head, distant and unreal.

Then he was being shaken. Shaken in a vigorous, sleep-destroying manner. His head was flopping backward and forward like a half filled rag doll. He longed to deny the violence, to ignore the attempt to draw him back, to disturb, and to make him get up. He wanted to sleep and ignore the distant voice that he could hear vaguely and indistinctly.

"Get up. Get up. You can't lie here. You'll drown. The tide is on the turn."

"Leave me alone. I beg you." His head fell on one side as though there was nothing firm to hold it erect.

"The tide is on the turn."

"Leave me alone, I beg you," he repeated.

Emma tried to drag him but his waterlogged body moved fractionally and then relaxed into a contorted, impassive heap. It did not respond to her frantic cries of distress. Overhead the sea birds wheeled and dived. She could see the tidal waves thundering up the beach. They were taller than her - huge white crested waves that lurched toward her and winged high in the sky before they broke in surf and thundered on the beach.

Kyoto was being thrown further and further away from her by the sea. The beach shelved from a raised platform ridge of pebbles, and the tide circled around the rocks in an alarming fashion. The plaque of sand they were on was getting smaller and smaller and flung spray covered it completely at times. Emma reached out and grasped a handful of Kyoto's clothing. There was no time to be gentle and patient. She held on to his arm and dragged on it with all her might.

"Do something for yourself. Get up! Get up! We are going to be cut off by the tide. I beg you to get up."

The wind and the noise of the incoming tide threw the words away from her. "Kyoto," she shrieked, as the circle of sand became smaller and smaller as another wave circled around the rocks and a sideward tidal current met the straight waves coming on to the beach and threw spray up into her face.

Then she heard the sound of splashing. Someone was wading out towards them, wading out from the raised beach. She raised her head and there before her was a man.

19

Scan joined up with his followers and they resolutely made their way towards the light which they could see ahead of them in the distance. Then they heard a noise like the thunder of an approaching express train.

"Whatever can it be?" said one of the men.

The noise echoed through the narrow tunnels bouncing back from one wall to the other.

"It sounds like water," another man answered in a doubtful, fearful way. "It reminds me of the time I was with another man in a swallow hole, out on the limestone workings, when we heard a noise. I was trying to remember where I'd heard that sound before. It was a long time ago and it was underground. I was told afterward that during heavy surface rain, the commons and higher ground drain down and carve holes through the limestone. The ground is riddled with underground tunnels cut by this continual water movement. It all gravitates towards lower ground and eventually reaches the sea, coming out on the beach as a fresh water stream. That's what the noise is I'm sure. I was told that I'd been fortunate to get out alive."

"We'll be drowned," said another man in a faltering voice. "We don't stand a chance. If these tunnels fill with water we'll drown I tell you."

He looked upward at the towering columns, where the slow drip, drip of water had formed massive stalagmites and stalactites which had joined in the middle to form gigantic columns which arched like a fanned cathedral up into the roof of the cave.

Scan followed his gaze. "Look," he said. He pointed to some indentations in the wall of rock. "Can you see what I see?"

"There's no time for standing still. I'm not interested in what you can see up there," the frightened man grumbled hysterically. "We're in danger, man."

"Listen to what I have to say," said Scan. He climbed upward to a ledge, four, five feet above the base of the tunnel. He held a green fern in his hand. "If this can grow here it means the height of the water reaches a stable level which is not generally exceeded."

He held out his hand to the next man to him and helped him up on the ledge alongside where he stood. There was a grotto of green ferns growing on the moist walls and up above was a narrow outlet which was like a chimney, and through this opening, light filtered into the darkness.

"I reckon we'll be safe here," he said.

Even as the words were out of his mouth the thunder of water grew closer to where they were.

"Quick! One after the other," said Scan and they helped each other on to the out-jutting piece of rock. Then the water was upon them, surging and swirling along the passageway that they had been making their way along.

"I can't hold him. Help me somebody," said an anguished voice. Ready hands reached out to assist the last man from the floor of the cave to the ledge. He was being dragged to safety, when the buoyancy and power of the water dragged him out of their grasp and the last they saw of the man was an outstretched arm reaching out to them. Then his cries and the echo of his fear were gone into the darkness and there was no sign of him.

There was silence. Then their misery was broken by the rending snap of a bridge of rock across which several of them had clambered to make more room on the lower ledge. It crashed and fell like a biscuit broken in two when dunked in tea and then disappeared into the flood. It sank.

It was washed away.

"We're stuck. We'll never get down from here. The side of the rock face is too smooth," said one man.

"For the moment we are safe," said Scan. "While you have been talking I have been watching the level of the water. It has started to drop and has stabilised a foot and a half beneath the ledge we are on."

"We'll be in trouble if there is more flash flooding due to surface rain."

"That is true but looking at the signs of life flourishing in the half light it makes me sure that it does not happen very often. I don't think we have a lot to worry about."

"Perhaps it is not surface rain, it tastes salty, like sea water. I don't know what to make of it."

"Perhaps we are nearer to the sea than we realise and at high tide it fills with sea water. It is just possible it's a cave shaped by the sea."

"I don't think so. But if what you surmise is true we are stuck here for six, eight hours at least until the tide turns, and then, dependent on how far we have to go to get out in the open, we should make it at low tide when the tunnel should stay dry for the equivalent amount of time, if the distance isn't too far."

"Now, I don't want to lose anyone else, so I suggest we rope together. Biggest and anchor man in front and back and the smallest in the middle. If the water does hit us suddenly, the smallest ones are first to climb to safety. Have you got it? Right!"

"I'll be glad when we reach the outside, with sun above and the grass underfoot."

"So will I."

"And I," muttered another voice.

"Underground may be all right for dwarfs and trolls, but not for me." He paused momentarily. "What was that?"

It was the tap, tap, tap of a metallic object, metal on metal.

"It comes from behind this face of rock," said Scan. "Directly in line with where we are now."

"Tap, tap, tap." A sweet, thin voice sang clearly in a light pitched tone.

"Here we tap for elfin gold.

Yellow gold.

Tap, tap, tap.

Here we tap.

Here we tap.

Tap, tap, tap.

For elfin gold."

There was silence and the men looked from one to the other in a puzzled, apprehensive way.

"Who do you suppose it is?"

"It's not one of us playing a joke, having us on?" said one of the men, suspiciously.

"I don't think so," said Scan. "There could well be others down here as well as ourselves."

"The water is falling," said one man. "The level has dropped by a couple of inches. I've been watching it carefully."

"You're right. You can see quite clearly the original level of the water. There's a dark line," and as they watched the water was visibly falling lower and lower.

"We'll have to gauge how deep it is and then drop down one at a time to the floor of the tunnel. We'll have to use the rope."

"But that means that one man will be stranded."

"I've thought of that," said Scan. "Anchor the length of the rope around that rock with an axe, then the last to get down can let himself down the rope to the floor."

"That means we'll lose the rope and the axe."

"There's nothing else we can do."

20

The five cats sat in an impassive row. Then their ears flattened and they crouched lower on the ground, growling low in their throats. Then five paws lashed out together at David. Cruel claws extended, dug deeply into his skin.

"You dare to provoke the anger of Xylo," they growled low in their throats and spit and snarled at David. "Mind your ways," and they lashed out again with unsheathed claws. "Otherwise, we will shred you into minced meat. The anger of Xylo is growing. He is aroused by the way you act, and will not be slow to retaliate and humiliate you if your ways are not changed."

They miaowed angrily and growled once again low in their throats and the bat like creatures flapped their wings aggressively and spread their talons and opened their mouths wide and hissed through their sharp, needle shaped teeth.

David crouched back in terror.

"You do well to be frightened," and they advanced closer to David. David moved back several feet. The cats, sable as night, with dense, black fur standing aggressively on end moved forward.

David moved backward.

They moved forward.

David backward.

Forward.

Backward, until David felt the hardness of rock firm behind him, and he flattened his body as closely to it as possible. In his heart he wished he could merge with the hard substance. To flee from before the amber eyes which seemed to be growing and growing like massive candle flames, until before him were only amber orbs, smouldering with hate and anger, coming closer and closer, so close that David felt he was within the circular eye, a small figure looking back out through the opalescent lens of the eye; his fists flailing at the glass surface.

"I am David, David," he murmured.

They rushed at him and he felt the rough way he was handled by many uncaring hands, thrown from one to the other carelessly, unloving. Hands made for caressing, loving, for healing. Soft, gentle hands. Well-cared, well-manicured hands, to soothe the feeble brow, to magic away hurt, had changed into rough, callused, hard hands, hands which thrust away, that were clenched, hit, slapped, rejected, dragged. He was drawn like a sack of potatoes along the corridors. He heard the sound of a key grating in a lock and then he was thrust headlong into the darkness.

Then silence, a long protracted, drawn out silence. Timeless silence.

"Are you all right?" said a voice. "Is that David?"

David felt emotionally emptied and depleted and could not answer.

"You are with friends. There's nothing to be frightened of."

Still he could not find his voice. Perhaps it had been taken away and he was effectively dumb and would never speak again. Anyway how could he tell if they were friends? They only said they were. There was no proof or evidence. Perhaps this was another trick, another way of taking him over. These evil servants of Xylo would stop at nothing to gain their ends.

"Here rest on my shoulder," said a voice. "It is broad and strong. You will soon feel better." He put his arms around David.

David angrily shrugged it off. "My name is David," he

reaffirmed in a voice that he was surprised to hear.

"Steady, steady. I mean you no harm," said the man and added "We do not forget the help you gave us when we were unhappy and in low spirits. Now let us help you."

"How can I tell that this is not a set up, and I will be made vulnerable by your kindness and then caught out?" He hesitated. "The followers of Xylo are everywhere, listening, ears cocked attentively, waiting for signs of weakness, ways in which I betray myself and they are on the ready to take over and make me one of theirs." He sobbed piteously. "I need friends. I want to be understood."

Then he fell into the man's open arms that drew him tightly towards him. He felt enclosed surrounded by a warm, accepting embrace. David sobbed, "I see them all the time. Cats in a row with angry flicking tails and claws which lunge out, tearing and scratching." He buried his head deeply into the clothes of the man that held him, a man who crooned gently and whispered soothing words of comfort.

"Rest gently, sleep sweetly. All is well. Tall grasses swing in the breeze. The sun is warm. All is well. Rest sweetly. Sleep gently. All is well. All is well."

David knew that he was trying to keep awake, to overcome the tiredness which he found difficult to resist. To stay aware, just in case of danger, but his resistance was proving difficult to maintain. The caring and gentleness was having the desired effect. He could resist it no longer. Then he gave in and allowed his senses to drift off, to lose contact with his conscious self. The suffering physical self rested still and quiet in the arms of the man who had befriended him.

"That is good," said the man. "Rest is what he needed, to renew his physical and spiritual energies." He looked at the still, quiet face. "He is drained, empty, and this point of crisis is a danger point." He sat quietly for a moment or two and then resumed in a hushed, quiet voice. "If they had pressed him one degree harder they would have had him.

Not often do the followers of Xylo make a mistake like this. They are adept at summing up the breaking point of each individual. Even now he is vulnerable, but sleep is the great restorer of health and mental stamina. He is overstrained and highly strung at the moment but his natural resilience will assert itself and his spirit will be renewed."

"The time has come to plan," said another voice. "We cannot rot in this fetid dungeon. Let us plan to escape."

"Escape from here? You must be joking. Do you know where you are?"

"I know we have good on our side and that we have accepted too readily that we have no control over what is happening to us. We have been too compliant, too ready to accept our helplessness."

"It is like escaping through the eye of a needle." The man sounded as though he was table thumping as he said in a monotonous, monotone voice. "Xylo is all powerful, dominant, supreme. What chance have we to change his plans for us?"

"But the thread a spider spins is delicate and thin, but it holds its weight," said a voice. "Gossamer. It looks as though it is going to snap but it sways in the wind and carries the spider from flower to ground."

"That may be."

"However slender our hopes, they could effectively carry us to safety, so planning is good."

"To make use of what we have planned would be even better," said another voice plaintively.

"The wind cool on my face. The sun warm on my neck."

"Yes let us plan to get out of this damp, dirty hole. Even thinking about doing something to help ourselves is making me feel better."

21

Emma waved enthusiastically to the stranger on the beach. He answered with a wave. Emma cupped her hands to her mouth, so that the words she shouted would be amplified and made louder.

"We are in great danger. The sand is unstable and if you put one foot from where you are you will sink to the waist. The quicksand will not take your weight. Do not move. Stay where you are."

She heard in her mind reassurance and the following words. "I will reach you. Do not take any action."

She yelled out "Do you hear what I say? Stay where you are. You cannot help me. If you understand what I am trying to tell you, raise both your hands above your head and bring them together."

This the man did.

"Right, stay where you are. There is no point in anybody else being put in danger. There is nothing you can do."

Emma watched the man disappear around a rocky outcrop. Her spirits dropped to zero level. He wasn't going to do anything stupid. The current was running fast and even a strong swimmer would not survive in these conditions. The mighty surf was raining down on her and rapidly narrowing the piece of sand on which she stood. She was wet to the skin and the salty water was washing all over her and making her clothes heavy and uncomfortable. Kyoto was still not aware of what was happening around him. She wondered if he was still alive. His body was in danger of drifting out on the current. It rose and fell on the incoming tide. Emma lunged forward and grasped the material of his over shirt and held on to it.

The sand she was standing on was becoming saturated and small bubbles were oozing up to the surface, as though alive with small sand creatures but it was the water infiltrating through the unstable sand. Her feet were sinking deeper and she found difficulty in pulling them out. She had lost her shoe; it had been sucked from her foot by the suction of the sand and water.

The sea lashed in an irregular wall, as though suspended by some unseen force, and it hung high above her as though she was in the trough and the crest any moment would come thundering down upon her.

*　　*　　*

Scan was in the process of organising the next step to take when one of his followers said, "I think you're forgetting one thing. There is no need for us to follow the ground level of the tunnel. If you look upwards the light we have seen is filtering in from above. There must be some way to the surface in that direction."

"There could be problems associated with climbing upwards through this chimney." He was looking up and flashing his light to assess what the surface was like. "It looks sheer and difficult to climb. I think we could have a problem finding footholds and anywhere to hold on to with our hands. Looks difficult and a hard climb to me."

They all peered upward.

"This mountain is riddled with holes and tunnels. There are probably passage ways fanning off in all directions," the man added. "The ferns could only grow where there was light. If you look upward it looks like a natural chimney to the surface. We're not as deeply underground as we thought."

"That's right but you're ignoring the fact that the surface is sheer and will prove impossible to scale without proper equipment."

"My ears and buttons," said a small, thin voice. "What have we here?" Standing at Scan's elbow was a miniature, elfin man dressed all in green. "You dare to intrude into the underground kingdom of we folk. Fal de rol! Big trouble awaits those who come with greed in their hearts and seek to steal and cause hardship and hurt."

"All we seek is a way to the surface, to the dark, star-studded sky and the breeze, cool on our faces. We wish you no harm. On the contrary we seek your help."

"We are on a quest to reach the Plain of Sol, to prevent evil spreading its power in our country. Time is important to us and we are lost and delayed in our journey. Forgive us this intrusion. Our bumping into you was an accident. We have no hidden motive."

"Perhaps what you say has the ring of truth, but so many people come with one thought and that is to steal our elfin gold."

"We have no intention of doing that," said Scan. "But if you could put us on the right track, we will be on our way."

"I have a feeling," said the elfin man, "that you are they who are spoken of in the chronicles. They will arrive on the way to Tingate Well and will ask your help." He looked querulously at them. "Could it be you and your companions who are mentioned in this way?" There was no answer. "It is written that peace and prosperity will come to the people of Thanbodia by the intercession of this person. Could this be one of you?"

"Sadly she is not with us. We became separated when we were attacked. We are concerned for her safety."

"I feel your sadness," said the elfin figure with compassion. "But you still have to follow your path with hope in your hearts and the knowing that fate will bring you together again to fulfil your purpose. Follow me," he added and this they did with new optimism and strength.

He went ahead of them down the narrow passage through which they had to move in a doubled up fashion because the roof was low, and then the tunnel opened into a large cave, lit with light which flickered in a movement of kaleidoscopic hues and colours which were unlike anything that they had seen before. There were ledges piled high with baskets of gold, articles and objects engraved with great artistry and love. There were goblets, shallow platters, deep tureens, cups, daintily figured with leaves and flowers, the oak leaves and acorns in a delicate skein, fit to grace the table of a king. The small elfin man showed them a favourite of his engraved with great artistry and attention to detail. It was a dish with a lid engraved with wood anemones, celandines and wild garlic interlaced with bluebells, engraved and enamelled with great skill and care.

Scan picked it up and fingered the beautiful, patterned surface with reverence clear to see.

"You like it," said the elfin man. "Then it is yours to keep into perpetuity. A memento of a meeting." He held it out to Scan. "Please accept it."

"Thank you," said Scan. "It will remind me of you and of your existence."

"It will do more than that. Hold it close to you. It has been inspired and forged with great love."

"It is time we got underway. We have delayed too long. I suspect we need to clear the tunnel before the tide turns."

"There is no need for your apprehension. We know this underground area like the back of our hands."

They felt the warmth of reassurance and knew that they were in safe hands and that no danger could come to them at this time. They would soon be out of these never ending underground passages. They followed the man dressed in elfin green, as he led them with light, dancing footsteps through the moist, wet, slippery tunnels. The stones were slimy and treacherous underfoot and this slowed down their progress.

The little man sang melodically and sweetly. His elfin voice rang like a crystal, clear and cold.

"Through the tunnels trip, trip, trip.

Tip your toes, tip, tip, tip.

On we go. On we go,

Through the tunnels on we go.

Follow the elfin folk. Follow where they go.

Follow where they go.

Through the tunnels dark and damp,

Through the tunnels dark and damp,

To the light. To the light.

Through the tunnels to the light."

They bobbed ahead in a line of moving lights that cast strange shadows on the walls that reflected the sparkle of crystal and jewels on the surface of the rock abraded to a shine by the continual flow and movement of water. It was beautiful and unlike anything that they had seen before. They had seen many unbelievable sights but this would always take pride of place in the memory of their journey.

The sound in the distance of the incoming tide, the boom and the rattle of surf breaking on pebbles and the sucking, hissing sound as the water was drawn back through the stones as they rose and closed up on each other, was getting noisier and noisier.

Then they were out in the daylight. Before them the giant breakers crashing relentlessly on the sand and rocky shore. And a figure stranded on a strip of sand which even as they watched was becoming smaller and smaller. Scan, even as he recognised the figure, was running, running hands upraised in acknowledgement.

"Stay where you are. Do not move."

It was Emma and his heart swelled with hope and love. He had found Emma. Their separate paths had come together again. The elfin men looked from one to the other.

"These are quake sands. They take and never give back.

153

The people of this land used to punish wrongdoers. The sand was their judge. If the person were blameless the sand would eject them. If they were guilty they disappeared, never to be seen again."

Scan stopped abruptly as the words registered in his mind and, as he withdrew his feet, the sand visibly quaked and moved and a deep gouge in the sand showed where his last footsteps had been. It filled with water and then disappeared

"Emma is in very great danger what can we do to help her?"

"Never fear," said one of the elfin men in answer to Scan's question. "We have long been acquainted with these sands. There is a way through. A ridge of rock runs from the cliff. The outcrop reaches under the sand and ends on the area where Emma is standing. There is not a moment to spare if we are to reach her before the tide claims the narrow strip of beach upon which she is standing."

The intensity and fury of the water was gaining momentum. It was filling the cove with a surging torrent of circular movement which foamed and fretted against the needle sharp rocks which stood like sentinels around the entrance to the network of tunnels they had so recently made their way through. Could they reach her in time or was it already too late?

22

David felt bruised mentally and physically. For a moment he couldn't place where he was. And then the terror of what had happened came back to him in a rush.

"Where am I? Where am I?" He yelled and lashed out in the darkness.

"Steady on. Steady on now. Everything's all right. I have you safe," said a kind, supportive voice.

David lashed around in an agony of anxiety and fear.

"There, there. You are back with us. You have slept the clock around and it will have refreshed you and brought you new courage."

David thought you are trying new tactics; the gentle approach. It won't work. He felt rebellion and resistance rising up in him like a flood. They weren't going to get him. No way!

"I am David," he repeated. "Do you hear me? I am David."

Still the silence.

"I am David!" he reiterated in a still louder voice, just in case they hadn't heard him before. Then his eyes noticed the faint hint of daylight through the grille high in the wall.

"I am David," and his voice became scarcely audible. "David, David," and he stared up at the slight difference in light with a stirring of memory. Perhaps he was back in the dungeon. "They will be back for me," said David. "I heard them say leave it for today, we'll work on him again tomorrow."

"Now listen. We have a plan. We must thwart what

they have in mind."

"We will never get out of here. These walls are solid, the door is strong and thick and the only window," David looked up at the grilled gap through which a grey light filtered, "is high in the wall."

"We have planned through the night and the mere act of making escape plans has made us come to life, to lose some of our helplessness and apathy. Be positive David. Look to the future."

"There is no future. Enough the day to live through, without thinking of endless days without any hope."

"You encouraged us when we felt depressed and low in spirits. Now it is our turn to make you see that we can make our own future. It is in our hands. It is our birthright to find an alternative way out of a situation."

David felt the tears obscuring his vision, so that the face in front of him was an indistinct blur and then the release of the tears as they overran and trickled down his cheeks allowed him to see again the caring, kind face that was looking at him with deep concern.

"It is as though we have come to life. We have something to live for." He put his arm around David's thin shoulder. "Now, listen to what I have to say, David boy. No don't pretend that you are not crying, there's nothing to be ashamed of. I know you have been brought up with the idea that to cry is unmanly, but this is a cultural thing. In other parts of the world it would be counted as unfeeling not to express a deep emotion when it is felt. You need to accept that you are compounded of male and female and it is good to cultivate the nurturing, tender side of your personality as well as the protective and assertive. If you cannot express how you feel, how can you expect to put yourself in the place of the other person and understand how they are feeling?"

"I was told when I was growing up that big boys don't cry, that it was sissyish to cry, that only girls cry."

"I feel for you. Now you know that this is not true. About this plan."

They huddled together and from the whispered voices, David pieced together what they were going to do.

The sound of footsteps outside in the corridor and the jangling of keys broke up their discussion. They heard the sound of the key turning in the unoiled lock and the metal stay which reinforced the outside of the door was removed and thrown down on the stone floor in the corridor.

The men inside the dungeon hissed, "It is now or never. Get yourselves ready for action. You, Set, behind the door and be ready to back up Set if he has difficulty in dealing with the man. Be ready to support his attack and wait for the signal to put the second part of the plan into action. You'll hear a low whistle like this."

"Right."

They watched with taut, anxious expressions as the door opened inward. Then the unexpected happened. A frightened, half delirious voice yelled out. The cry hung in the air, tense, expectant and was followed by a long drawn out groan of pain.

"I can't take any more of this. Don't let them find me. Hide me from them."

A whip lashed out, eating into the bodies of the people huddled on the floor.

"We come for him called David. He is here, we are well aware of that fact. It is no time for games."

The whip lashed out again with ferocious savagery. "You will all suffer if you protect and hide him." The whip lashed out again, cutting deep into their flesh of the vulnerable men. And making the resentment inside them burn with an overpowering sense of injustice and injury.

"If you do not come willingly we will have to hunt you out like an animal. There is no avoiding the retaliation of Xylo. You will give in. You will beg for mercy by the time we have finished with you. Take heed of our words."

"I will not come with you. How can you catch someone who is not here?" His laughter rang out in an unstable, maniacal way and reverberated through the dark interior of the prison cell.

"I am not here. I have never been."

"When you feel this whip then you will realise the solidity of flesh and its frailty. I command you to get up and come here. If you ignore our warnings you will suffer the torments of hell before we drain the last dregs of that part of you that you remember as David. Your soul will be filled with terror before we finish with you. You will beg to do the will of Xylo. You will plead for the last dregs of what you were to drain through the colander of time and to allow you the peace of forgetfulness, of not knowing who you were. You will then be in our power. A servant of Xylo. Your whole body will yearn to do the will of Xylo. You will plead to do anything he says. You will kneel to him, bow your head to him and do what he says without question, whatever it may be."

'When will he stop?' thought David.

The voice went on.

"Then you will pay for your disobedience. You do not know what is before you."

The lash of the whip rained down on the men as, frustrated by lack of success and burning with anger, they moved forward among the prisoners. They had always been told not to do this, to keep their distance, to stand off, but this time they forgot their orders, incensed by the rebellious attitude of the prisoners. All they wanted to do was make these men conform, do as they were told.

Too late they realised the trap they had fallen into. They struggled to throw off the hands around their throats and to yell out for help, but the cry ended in a gurgle of shut off words, and then silence.

The man at the door called in a frightened way "Are you all right?"

Then in answer to the arranged whistle, there was a movement of feet and then the voice was no more. There was the scuffle of noise. A low moan and the resultant silence broken by the words "We've done it."

There was a subdued cheer.

"Not too loud. We do not want to attract attention. They will know soon enough that something is wrong. Drag the bodies deep into the dark of the dungeon so that they will not readily be noticed. That's right. Take their keys. Take their keys." And he added "We may well need them if we are to reach safety."

He pointed a finger at two of the men. "Take their clothes and put them on. The tallest, they should be the better fit." He looked around him at the men. "There is no time to lose. Let us get on the other side of this door and lock and bar it. We're on the outside this time."

"Good feeling," said one of the other men. "It feels really good."

*　　*　　*

As though by a miracle, Scan was standing alongside Emma on the narrow strip of sand into which their feet were sinking deeper and deeper.

"There is no time to lose. We are both in great danger. The sand is waterlogged and soon you will not be able to release your feet. They will go on sinking until your whole body sinks under the sand."

Emma seemed oblivious to his words. She clung on to him, grasping him to her.

"I am safe with you," she said and tears of joy ran down her cheeks. Suddenly, Emma came to her senses. She remembered the danger she was in and she also remembered with an indrawn breath of anguish that in her moment of joy she had forgotten Kyoto. How could she do such a thing? It was unbelievable. "Kyoto, Kyoto." She screamed in anguish and pain. "Kyoto," she cried again and again to the empty sky and the sea covered sand. "Kyoto, Kyoto," but the only answer was the melancholy mewing of a lone seagull.

There was no answering response to her anguished cry.

"We have come so far together. I cannot lose you now. Help is at hand, so near and yet so far for you," she mumbled. There was a cruel irony in what had happened. His companionship, his dependency and need had kept her going in the face of trauma and difficulty. His unspoken need of her had given an incentive not to give up when her whole body had cried out for release from the situation.

Where was he? Then, hadn't he told her that his purpose was to bring Scan and Emma back together again and hadn't he fulfilled that purpose beyond all hopes.

She looked at Scan. "He brought us back together and that was his aim." She remembered nostalgically how he had reinforced her conviction that she had to fight her way through to accomplish the prophecy. She had an important task in front of her that was her destiny.

"Kyoto. Kyoto," she sobbed, but her words were lost in the tidal fury, as the water poured in a torrent through the underground caves with an eerie sound that echoed in her ears. It sucked and seethed and whistled incessantly. A thunder of fury.

She tried to drag her feet out of the sand but they would not come free. She was stuck, unable to move. This was the end. She collapsed into the arms of Scan in a deep state of unconsciousness.

*   *   *

The underground stone passageway was damp and disagreeable. The smell of unwashed bodies and sweat was less than in the enclosed dungeon but there was green moss and slime everywhere and water oozed down the walls and dropped down from the roof of the tunnel. There was the smell of fungal decay and rotting.

A brand of light was set in the walls at regular intervals that lit up the tunnel in irregular pools of light.

"This way," and with silent footsteps they followed one after the other, cautiously, furtively alert for a sign of the enemy. All was still except for the continuous drip of condensation from the grim, cold walls and the splutter of the brands as water threatened to put them out. David shuddered involuntarily as though someone was walking across his grave. He was frightened.

"You'll be all right, Davie boy. We'll get out of here, you'll see."

A flurry of water fell down on them from the roof.

"What is that noise?" said David. "It sounds like machinery." The vibration and noise made the floor pulsate and move as though there was an earthquake tremor.

"They are driving into the mountain, enlarging the area they have underground. The ventilation system, to purify the air, and the generators, to provide electricity are on all the time and they create a background hum of electrical noise. To live underground is a specialised environment that needs much engineering, planning and adaptation. They know what they are doing."

"Do you think we have a chance of survival?"

"Gerein here has a rough idea of the layout of the tunnels. He has worked here, been one of those who transport prisoners and supplies back and forward. He was a guard for a short time but refused to carry out an order and was thrown into the dungeon prior to being programmed all over again. No good to them as he was. They want docile, suggestive people who do as they are told without question. No free spirits here with a will of their own. They go for the easily crushed, the submissive who just do as they are told without a thought of the consequences, the outcome of their actions." He hesitated for a moment. "What is it Gerein?"

"Five hundred yards from this point there is a control box. It monitors the tunnels that lead to the exterior. The camera lenses are placed on a bracket and a view of the tunnel is on a monitor screen in the control room."

"Ought to be easy enough to cover them up and creep on all fours below the level of vision."

"That's as maybe. But they are clever. The cameras pivot and run on separate time sequences so there is always a view of upper, middle and lower areas at the same time."

"Put out the brands which give light, then we can cover the camera lens. They'll think there has been an electrical fault, a breakdown. That'll give us time to get through."

"Think up another one!"

"Why did you say that? Isn't the idea worth considering?"

Gerein shrugged his head. "They have orders. Any camera fault or technical difficulty and the screens come down and cut off, sectionise the corridor. I told you they were thorough and clever too. Until they find the cause of the problem the screens stay in position. I had friends who tried to get out that way, were caught in a pocket between two screen doors and had to wait there until the guards came for them." He shrugged his shoulders. "Last I saw of them."

"Could we prop the doors up at the bottom so that they stay clear from the ground for about a foot. This would give us space to crawl under and get to the other side," said another man.

"You're an optimist," laughed a further man in a scornful manner.

"It would be quite a task, the doors come down simultaneously."

"Where are the points where the screens are fixed?"

"There are three as you can see." He examined them in a cursory, superficial manner. "I agree, tricky, if not impossible."

"What other alternative have we got?"

"One thing for sure, we can't hang around here discussing the practicalities. They will soon be aware of our escape, that is if they haven't already found that out and then there will be a full scale alert."

He had noticed that several of the men were getting restless and jumpy and Gerein noticed their erratic glances over their shoulders to check if there was anybody creeping up behind them.

"Are there any ventilators, shafts, openings in the wall?"

"That's a good idea. I hadn't thought of that."

"If we could bypass the length of corridor," he put his hand to his chin thoughtfully. "What do you think? That looks like a ventilation opening. How accessible is it?" He looked critically at the metal plate. "If we could throw out the lower camera we could try and prise off the cover."

"I'm game for a try. The camera sweeps from left to right. We'll have to be quick to get behind it and throw a coat or something over the lens."

"Ay!"

"When I say right, off you go."

"Right."

With tense faces and indrawn breath they watched the man keeping low to the ground in order to keep out of the range of the camera.

"Done it. I can't believe it. He's done it. Hip hip hooray!"

The man held his hand in the air to let them know that he had succeeded and then moved higher up the corridor looking for the ventilator opening. It unscrewed easily and he gave the waiting, expectant men a thumbs up sign.

"He's done it. The alarm hasn't gone off. We're in luck's way."

The ventilator cover unscrewed from the wall without any difficulty and came off noiselessly into the man's hands. The shaft looked large enough to take a man of ordinary height in an upright position. It was dark and noisy but it would suit their purpose.

He gave another thumbs up sign and the tension of the waiting men visibly gave way to the indrawn breath of relief. Then the bell went off and the noise of its discharge echoed back from one wall to the other. The man by the ventilator shaft waved them on.

"Hurry, there's no time to lose. As quick as possible into the hole. The shaft will take us. Do not waste time. There is no time for delay."

In the distance they could hear the sound of quickly moving feet and the buzz of voices. They crouched uneasily in the darkened ventilator shaft. It was larger than they thought it would be. One of the men managed to hold the shaft cover in position, with obvious difficulty.

The purposeful rush of many feet made their way past where they were hidden. They stayed immobile, motionless, without movement until the noise had faded into the distance.

"I can't hold on to it any longer," said the man holding the shaft cover. "My fingers are going numb and any moment it is going to slip out of my grasp."

"It needs to be wedged, but can we do it from inside. There's a piece of wood here. Would that be of any use?"

"I'll have a try but I've got a feeling that it's not going to work. It's likely to fall into the corridor and then we'll be in trouble."

"The fixing screws need to be put in on the other side. Anybody got any ideas?"

"Try the wood. You never know, it may work."

"Careful! Careful! You'll have the thing out of my grasp," grumbled the man who was holding the metal plate.

"Keep quiet. There's something out there. Keep perfectly still."

Not daring to breath they listened attentively trying to

identify the unfamiliar sound. There were no footsteps. But there was something out there in the corridor, gliding smoothly, almost noiselessly past the ventilator shaft. What could it be? There was no way of satisfying their curiosity. There was no way of checking what was out in the corridor.

"You know," said Damian, one of the men. "It sounds like a... No, it couldn't be. Scientifically there was no chance that the people of Xylo could have progressed that far with their knowledge."

"But wait," said Zenda, "they absorb all the thoughts, the power, the knowledge of the people they catch. The knowledge is theirs without any personal thought or research. It is just possible that what you suspect is true. They could have caught one of the Mainlanders. And I fear the consequences if this is what they have learnt to do. A full scale atomic war could be unleashed on the universe."

A mutter of disbelief and abhorrence ran through the group of people.

"If this is true and they recognise what they have in their hands there is an even greater threat to our civilisation. They have only to lay their plans carefully and capture the right people with the right knowledge and they will be updated on all the new scientific experiments, equipment and locations, codes of missiles and everything else that is kept secret. Any newfound knowledge will be theirs. Then we will be in real trouble."

"As though we aren't already," said another man gloomily.

"For God's sake, do something about this shaft opening. I can't hold on any longer. It's starting to slip between my fingers. I'm going to drop it. No, not pushing it away from you. It'll fall on the corridor floor. Never mind about scientific observations and philosophic discussion get here and give me a hand. It's going to look mighty suspicious if this thing drops right in front of one of the guards. They'll soon be on to what we are trying to do." He carried on in an impatient tirade of anger. "Do get off my foot. No don't do it that way, that'll be no good. There's nothing for it. I'll have to get back down in the corridor and screw the ventilation cover back on. At least the greatest majority will not be in such acute danger. I'll manage, somehow, to get through and meet up with you again."

"You don't stand a chance. We need to stick together. No heroics."

"There's no alternative. Let's toss for it. That'll be fair. Heads it's me, tails it's you."

"Look, I know the layouts of the tunnels and if anybody is going to get through it will be me," said Gerein. "Remember I used to work for Xylo until I fell foul and went against something he asked to be done, was going to be programmed again but they never got around to it."

He slipped through the ventilator shaft and put the cover back up against the hole. The men listened to him screwing the retaining screws into position. They heard his footsteps recede into the distance.

"So far, so good," said one of the men.

They started to move cautiously along the inner tunnel. Whatever had been out there in the corridor had moved away. It was no threat to them at the moment.

"If you hear anything freeze, wait and keep still. Noise will give us away and attract attention."

They were making quite good progress when they heard the monotonous, one note tone of mechanical speech. Another responded in the same way. It was a continuous line, without inflexion, without the usual cadences of human talk.

"He is unable to find out where we have gone. He is reprimanding them for lifting the sectional, cut off doors too soon, giving the prisoners the chance to escape. The cave area is outside Xylo's control so that's our objective. Listen!"

"They will not reach the upper surface. Never fear!"

"They will never break free of the darkness. They are as surely imprisoned as if they were behind a locked, barred door."

"Never fear! Never fear! Never fear! Never fear!"

"Sounds as though a circuit has stuck."

"You've hit it on the nail," said Damian. "It sounds as though Xylo has come to grips with the science of robotics. Those voices, as I thought, are robots, advanced robots patrolling the section from the dungeon to the outer world."

"What chance will Gerein have of reaching safety?"

"He has to contend with electronic surveillance systems, microchips and the like."

"I was totally unprepared to find this advancement in their civilisation. They are strides ahead of parts of the world. As we said before, the feedback they get from the people they catch is automatically fed into their computer files. It is possible that they are already identifying people whose knowledge will be useful to them and kidnapping them in order to further the branch of learning which they want to enlarge and widen. And there is no need to say any more. We are all aware of the power and dictatorship which is crippling our people."

There was silence for a moment or so as the realisation of what could happen in the future hung heavily over them. David shrugged the depressive state off purposefully. There was no point in this negative, destructive thinking. They were still alive, and in that lay hope.

"We are delaying too long. We may think that we are safe but how long do you think it's going to take before they think of checking the ventilation shaft? We are still in a perilous position and I think it best if we leave the ins and outs of the situation to discuss until we are free."

"Not a bad idea by my reckoning. There's always the risk that if Gerein is captured, he will break down and give away our hiding place. There's a limit to what the body and mind can stand under torture"

"Where do we break through into the main tunnel? This shaft seems to go on forever. We've covered quite a distance."

"This lack of progress sits heavily on my shoulders," said Damian. "We seem to be getting nowhere."

"There must be something to learn from this," said another man in a philosophic way. "That's life. It often seems that we are getting nowhere, but really it is a time of assessment, like being on a plateau surveying the situation, but none the less change is always happening."

"Baloney!" said David, rejecting what he thought was an adult viewpoint of the world. "I don't want to know."

"That's right, tell them David. If I'd known we had a bunch of philosophers I would have checked credentials before we started. We want practical, technical support."

"You want to hide your head under a blanket, like you used to when you were a child. The bedclothes right over your head when you were frightened of the dark, and all the time you thought you were covered and safe and your feet were sticking out at the bottom of the bed."

"You're wrong there. I used to keep a little gap so that I could see what was going on."

"It would be a good idea if you came back to what's happening around you at this present moment in time."

"It's time for decisions, decisions. Perhaps for taking risks. I've noticed that the ventilator openings are getting fewer and more widely spaced. I've been trying to work out the reason for this."

"Do you think it means that we are coming to the end of the shaft and we'll come up against a solid wall?"

"It's possible. Then we'll have to get back to the last hole and aim at getting out at that point. It makes sense."

"Is it possible that that area will be more heavily patrolled? That's where the risk comes in."

"Well, what steps do we take? Do we break out higher up the tunnel and make our way towards the boundary line or do we get as far as we can and then take the chance and deal with any opposition?"

There was silence. Nobody wanted to take responsibility for the outcome of whatever action was taken.

"What do you think, David?"

"I'm only..." David hesitated. He did not want to be considered a child, but he felt indecisive and threatened. Why should he take responsibility for what happened? Then, wasn't making decisions part of growing up? Ultimately taking responsibility for yourself, and if necessary the other, weaker person? "I'm afraid," he said openly with a surprising candour. "I'm frightened of making a decision."

"So am I."

"And I," mumbled the rest, one after the other.

"Well, what can we do to help ourselves find the best thing to do?"

"Turn inward and ask that inner part of yourself for help, enlightenment."

"Like prayer," said a voice in the darkness.

There was quiet and stillness for a time as each man tried to sink into himself and find an answer to his predicament.

23

Scan and Emma sat on the cliff, resting in the sweet scented grass. A skylark went up and up, until it was a dot high in the sunny sky. Emma watched the dot becoming smaller and smaller, but she could still hear the clear notes of its song. The whistling echo from the caves had stopped. The cove was filling like a well. Emma wondered if the water would keep on rising until it reached the top of the cliff. She mentally pictured herself barefooted, dangling her toes in the water. Just a pinch of mustard added to soothe tired, aching feet. The absurdity of the picture made her giggle to herself. If they were caught in heavy rain on the way home from school, her mother, after getting all the wet clothes off, would wrap her in a large, warm towel and put newspaper on the floor to protect the rug, and then bring in a steaming bowl of mustard water to soak cold feet back to warmth.

A nostalgic hunger for home burned deep in the pit of her stomach. An ache of longing and desolation for the separation from her family. Scan burst in on her melancholic reflections.

"There is a plain on the other side of this range of hills which we must cross before it is too dark."

Emma hauled her tired body off the grass. She ached in every muscle and bone. She longed to stay where she was, to give in to this tiredness, which made her eyelids involuntarily close on her cheek. To stay awake was painful. Her body swayed dizzily as she stood upright. She nearly fell to the ground.

"Steady," said Scan, supporting her until she had regained her balance. "You are tired. We must find somewhere to rest as soon as we gain the other side of the valley. Can you manage a little longer? Here lean on me."

Emma felt her strength returning as though she was getting nurturing and sustenance from his closeness. A warm radiance seemed to surround her and a peaceful aura of happiness.

"I feel better," she said.

"The elfin folk have promised to accompany us as far as the outskirts of the Plain of Sol. The mountains are treacherous and peopled with wild races that maim and kill. They attack and slay without discrimination. They do not wait to see whether you are friend or enemy. They guard the mountain passes and kill those who venture into the mountains. The time must come when we stop these bandits from reigning with terror, and open up these valleys to the traveller. So many people have lost a father or son when peacefully travelling across these hills. It is sad, oh, so sad." He then added, "The time will come, but it is not yet right."

They climbed higher and higher and mist wuthered around them blowing in white skeins. It was cold and damp. A lone sheep looked up and stopped chewing the grass. His eyes slowly followed them as they scrambled along the rock strewn way. Then, as though bored with what he had seen, his head went back to cropping the grass.

A pocket of scree rocks fell down in a ripple of movement, narrowly missing the escarpment where they stood. Lower in the valley, the tops of the trees stood above a layer of cotton wool mist, strangely disembodied from their trunks and roots. Then an arrow, aimed at within a foot of Scan's leg, stopped their progress abruptly.

"To the shelter of the rocks," said a light, elfin voice.

"You dare to venture into the country of the Meni," said an abrasive, threatening voice. "Stand out in the open. Do as I say. Do you hear?"

A hail of arrows fell against the rock behind which they were sheltering.

"You do well to listen to the men of the Meni."

A giant of a man with rippling muscles moving in bands under the skin stood on an outcrop of rock above them. "You can do nothing. You are our prisoners."

They followed the direction of his glance. There, with arrows at the ready, was a massed army of men. They were tall and strongly made. Long, curly, black hair fell to the shoulder level. A black beard fell down on the black, matted chest. Their eyes were dark, intense and brooding. The fire of battle hung about them like a red aura of anger.

Then the anger changed to fear and they chattered noisily among themselves. Scan wondered what had caused the change in their mood. Then he saw a massed army of elfin figures surrounding the dark skinned giants in an arrow-shaped wedge of solid green. The Meni chattered in a frightened, agitated manner and cowered away from the elfin figures. Then, with further signs of fear, they retreated cat-like, belly to the ground, as though from a dominant animal, until they were hidden behind a ridge of rocks where with a defiant gesture they let loose a hail of arrows which sailed harmlessly up into the sky and over the heads of Scan and his followers.

Then the sound of tribal songs and repetitive dance rhythms, the beat of drums, made the Scan and his men feel fear.

"They will not attack you when we are here," said the elfin folk. "They fear the arrows which they think we shoot to bring them harm and illness. If their cows go dry or their cattle sicken and die, they blame it on the green people. They fear the power we elfin folk have been falsely rumoured to possess and will not risk arousing our anger. They do not want to lose face. Take courage, be of strong heart. Their show of tribal strength is to build up their courage. They are warding off harm."

They made their way through the outcrops of stone and stealthily past the Meni and on through the valley, down the wooded slopes to the floor, where a swift stream contoured its way, snake-like, as far as the eye could see. The undergrowth was dense.

On Scan's advice they hugged the valley floor and the slowly moving river until it opened out in a shallow ford crossed by a row of stepping-stones.

"We can go no further," said the elfin folk. "But to safely see you through the marshes on the other side of the river, one of us will go ahead and act as an ignuus fatuus." He saw their hesitancy and said, "A bright light will go ahead of you, to direct and guide you." He hastily reassured the people who were showing their anxiety by a low, disconcerted mumble of voices. "You see, even you have doubts about our integrity. It is not true that we lead people to their deaths. Do not fear. You will have to trust us. Follow the light and you will get safely to the other side. This we will do for you. Take heart. Be of good cheer. All will be well."

Scan and his men followed with great care the light, which danced a little ahead of them. It bridged hollows, hovered in the sky, darted ahead as though tired of progressing so slowly, then lunged back to where they were.

The ground was solid where they stood and their anxiety gave way to open confidence.

"We have always avoided this marsh. It has claimed many of our men," Scan said. "Obviously our fear was unfounded, like fear so often is."

Then, one of the men stumbled and the large pack that he was carrying on his back fell to the ground about two feet from where they stood.

"Wait! I had better get it otherwise we will be short of supplies."

He put a foot in the direction where the pack had fallen.

"Wait!" said Scan.

But the man was already knee deep in mud, which oozed around his body and was visibly pulling him down.

"Help me," he said and tried to lever himself upwards. This only worsened matters and he sank deeper into the bog.

"Do not struggle," yelled Scan. "Keep as still as you can." And he thrust a branch from an overhanging tree across the surface of the mud. "Hold on to that. It is your only chance of survival. If you struggle, it will suck you down still further. Do as I say."

The man reached out for the branch, but as his fingers closed over it, the greenery of the leaves pulled away and his body started to sink deeper and deeper, until only his head and shoulders could still be seen.

His eyeballs bulged in terror. "Help me! Help me!" and his frantic terror closed the mud over his head.

An outstretched arm was all that could be seen, and that slowly disappeared before the horror-filled eyes of the men that had travelled so far with him.

Scan shuddered involuntarily. "Remember well what you have seen. Let this be a warning to you. We were becoming too complacent and over confident. We need to exert caution."

The men silently looked at the spot where, a moment ago, there had been a man struggling for survival. A few marsh gas bubbles rose to the surface of the mud and disappeared into the atmosphere.

"Do not stray off the path of light. Even one footstep right or left could mean death."

The Will o' the Wisp of light rolled closer to them brightly illuminating the way ahead.

"Do as I say. We are safe when we stay within the light. If anything falls in the marsh make no attempt to retrieve it."

The followers of Scan concentrated intently on the way before them. They picked their way carefully forward.

"This marsh is bewitched," said one. "It is peopled by

the ghosts of the many who have died in the past. I'll be glad when I get to the other side, to the sorrel green Plain of Sol."

"The stench of marsh gas is in my nostrils and I am full of fear."

All this time Emma had been blanched with an unbelievable pallor that showed, only too clearly, the strain she was under. She could not take in; believe what she had just seen. One minute the man had been cheerful and in person before her eyes and then he was gone. Had sunk into the boggy marsh and nothing remained of him except a memory of that fear-wracked face, struggling to free himself, and the more he struggled the deeper and deeper he sank into the mud.

She cast a strained look at Scan and the emotion of what she had experienced showed vividly on her tense face. Her tiredness was making her walk unsteadily and she had to exert great care not to swing off the path. It was difficult for her to keep a straight line. Scan took her hand and held it firmly and comfortingly. Then the light, which was leading them, wrote words in the sky.

"Take comfort."

And then another sentence.

"You soon will be clear of this malignant, deadly marsh." And more. "Be of good cheer." Then another skein of words were outlined against the black of the sky. "When you see my glow no longer you are safely on the other side, on safe, firm ground."

It scattered more words on the blackboard of the night, the star-studded sky. "I say goodbye. Soon you will be safe. Be happy. May you prosper in all that you do, and may the power of good look favourably upon your cause." And then it was gone.

The ground was solid beneath their feet and a solitary owl hooted in the trees above their heads and the answering call rang out in the stillness of the night, and there was a movement in the bushes alongside them. The owl hooted again and the answering cry was nearer now, not as far distant as though it was homing in on the original call.

"Keep still," said Emma. "Did you hear? There's something in the bushes."

"It's probably a small creature hunting for food," said one of the men. "We're safe now, there's nothing to worry about."

The rustle of movement continued. "I'm frightened," said Emma. "Hold my hand and then I'll feel more confident."

24

David followed the others along the duct, which was getting narrower and narrower. He felt any moment it would peter out and they'd come up against a solid obstacle that there was no getting past. Then they would have to wriggle backward to where the tunnel widened.

The roof was damp, despite the air and heat that was circulating through the area, and condensation was dropping down upon them. They hit their heads every so often on the low roof and the floor was rough and uneven and scratched their knees and legs. Then, to their surprise, there was another ventilator in the wall, slightly larger than the others.

This puzzled Damian. "Why should it be larger than the others?" he said a frown furrowing his forehead. "I don' t understand the reason for it."

There was no further time for speech.

"Shush!"

"But…"

"I heard something," said Damian.

"I also," said David. "I heard it before. I was trying to make out what it was but I couldn't identify the sound above what we were saying."

"Shush!"

"Well, there's nothing there now, whatever it was."

The dark seemed to press down upon them. Every noise or movement seemed to be amplified by the silence.

"There."

"Is that you?"

They could not identify the voice so they kept silent

and listened intently for any further communication. Perhaps it was a way to get them to betray their presence. It could be that the enemy was unsure that there was anyone in the duct and they were testing to see if they got a response. Not a movement or sound betrayed them.

Then they heard the name, "Damian, Damian," repeated several times and then, "Damian do you hear me?" There was a brief silence broken by "It's Gerein. I've managed to stay free." Again silence. "If you push the metal plate to the shaft it'll fall outward. I've removed the screws."

Still the silence. "For heaven's sake let me know you can hear me. I've been waiting here until you reached this point." Still there was no answer. "Can't you hear me?" There was no further speech for a short time. Then his plaintive voice niggled again.

"What can I say to convince you that I'm on your side?" Then the unresponsive silence. And then his voice, irritable now as though he was losing patience with the situation. "There's no way I'm staying in this corridor any longer. In a short while the guards will be patrolling the area. I leave it to you." He continued, "What you do is your business."

They heard his footsteps receding down the corridor, until they could no longer hear them in the distance. The ventilator fell out as David pushed it and clattered on the floor. He put his head through the opening and looked both ways to check the corridor. It was empty, no movement or noise in the distance. The floor was of roughly hewn rock without any finish or lighting and the lit part of the corridor was like a circular gap beckoning in the distance.

As they thought, this must be the last ventilator. The shaft ended at this point. The larger opening must be used as an entry point for servicing and doing running repairs to the system.

They were all standing expectant and vulnerable

watching Damian replacing the screws in the panel. It was back in place now.

"We'd better not hang around if what Gerein said is true. I think we may well have misjudged him. He obviously knows this area well and is aware of the times that the guards can be expected to come down this end. If what he said has any meaning, we'd better move off."

"What if Gerein is one of them?" Could they depend on him or was he primed to lead them into trouble and servitude. It seemed so strange that he'd managed to stay free. The odds were stacked against him not being caught and yet here he was safe and sound. He was obviously annoyed with them but they'd talk him around and explain their reticence in letting anyone know of their whereabouts. He'd understand, Damian felt sure of this.

They hurried off in the direction away from the beckoning pool of light. He could not be far ahead. They would catch up with him and explain themselves. And there in the shadows they saw a flicker of movement as though some living thing was lurking in the darkness ahead of them.

They watched intently. But all was still now. No movement. No alteration in the blackness.

They crept silently forward, stumbling over the stones which had been left embedded in the roughly dug floor. It was so dark that the light they carried did not illuminate the ground enough for them to see where they were going and they tripped and fell several times and felt battered and bruised. Then they heard the rattle of stones coming down the slope towards them. Someone must be ahead, lurking in the shadows. The gradient was changing character. They must be climbing upward. Their legs ached with the effort of mastering the climb. Who was it in the darkness ahead of them?

And then a figure stepped out of the deeper shadows.

"Gerein!"

"I was hoping you would not be long in following," he said.

David gave a searching, questioning look at Gerein. "We thought you did not stand a chance and that it was the last we would see of you."

"Luck was on my side and, of course, my knowledge of the underground tunnels and the way they were patrolled. Mind you, they could have changed their routine and then I would have been in trouble but luck was with me. But there is no time to stand around. The soldiers of Xylo are even at this moment on their way to open the shaft."

"What has made them check the ventilation system?" said David. "Do they do this often?"

"They're not stupid you know! They must have realised that could be the only way you could have gone. People don't just disappear into thin air. You had to be somewhere. They think you are still in the shaft. They were all for sealing the ventilators and pumping in gas. When I heard them discussing this I realised what danger you were in." He stood quietly for a moment. "If you hadn't put in an appearance when you did, I was going to retrace my footsteps and try to locate where you were. When I heard your movements I was overcome with relief and joy."

"Until we refused to acknowledge that you were there. You deserve an apology," said Damian. "It must have been intensely frustrating to know we were there and not get an answer."

'Has he been taken over?' thought David. He seems the same Gerein they had always known. But then you could never tell. The one thing that that people who were taken over seemed to be adept at was the art of deception and substitution of deviousness for openness. Was this the true Gerein?

Gerein hugged them warmly. 'Is he one of them?' thought David, the persistent question intruding into his conscious mind. He registered the uncertainty on the faces of the other men. They felt the same as he did. They weren't sure. Didn't know what to make of the situation.

Then, he was openly emotional and responsive. Hadn't he greeted them warmly and with tears of joy and obvious delight? It must be Gerein. There was no need for this doubt and uncertainty. There was no question he was who he said he was. It was all in the mind.

"As I've said before, there is no time to stand around speculating," said Gerein. "I can hear the sound of many feet approaching."

"I suggest we go this way," said Damian.

"You do so at your peril. That tunnel is under surveillance. The robots patrol it on a regular basis and even now, if their time pattern is the same, they will be nearing this section."

"What do you suggest?" said David, the hot level of anger rising within him. Something was going to happen. They were even now under the supervisory eye of Xylo. They were being played with, like a cat plays with a mouse before it makes that final pounce and digs its claws into the warm flesh. He was letting them go so far and then putting something formidable in the way, then letting them move ahead again and then the obstacle. It was a cat and mouse game. Then, when they had enough of playing around, there'd be that final pounce which would mean death or captivity. David knew which one he would prefer. He shivered at the thought of what they were capable of.

Why did he have this recurrent, repetitive dream in which he was surrounded by water, rising water, filling up, cutting off, drowning, danger? Like a repeat run, the scene intruded into his mind without any reason, as though prompted by undercover, subliminal activity. Then, before he had widened his perception, it had gone as though it had never been. It left a residue of unease as though it was a premonition of what was to come, or some backdrop from the past.

In a half attentive way he directed his attention back to Gerein.

"You have to trust me," said Gerein as though he had suddenly identified a problem. "Where there is no trust there is no hope."

"Lead. Go ahead," said Damian. "We will follow you."

"This corridor is the best direction to take. It will lead to the inner core of the mountain where the rivers have hollowed, carved out underground caves and passages, the bed of old torrents that now flow on the surface of the land. Xylo's power is equal to ours in this outer region. Let us move as swiftly as possible so that the scales are balanced more equally."

They followed his form, which they could identify, easily by the phosphorescent glow that spread around him in the darkness.

"Seen that before in the surf beside the sea when it's dark," David said as he looked ahead at the figure of Gerein.

"On herring roes in the dark."

"It's strange. I've never noticed it before but in these underground conditions it makes it easier to see where he is."

Gerein knew that it was all meant. That he was to lead them to the Plain of Sol. It was a race against time. What had happened in the crystal cave where the meditators sat in their pyramidal shapes sending out healing, harmony and peace to the universe at large? Gerein knew he had never been the same since that day. Something that he could not explain had happened. The crystals had glowed with their particular colour offering to the world and Gerein had been immersed in their beauty, and for a time had lost touch with physical reality and had felt that ineffable sense of love and unity with all things. It was as though he had been drifting in deep space where there was no time, just depth, distance without end, stretching on and on into infinity.

Somehow it had changed his understanding. There had

been a remarkable change in his attitudes towards life. He felt renewed and strengthened. Different. He remembered what they had said to him. That Scan was ahead of them. That he also had visited the crystal cave. What had they said about the stone that had been given to Scan? It had been a crystal that had landed, meteor-like, from space and it had special powers and when the two moons met in the sky above the planet, their combined power would polarise at one point and this would influence the change in the vibratory rate to which the world would be exposed. It was of a yellow, gold colour, ridged with seams of deeper, translucent gold and copper lines streaked through it. The colour alternated, paled and deepened, as though it had a life of its own. It became cloudy and then crystal clear and the power that radiated from it drew your mind with a hypnotic intensity.

The copper of Gerein's hair seemed to glow in the dark like a beacon. David found his trust growing. Perhaps, after all, higher forces were leading them. To believe that all was well would bring its own dividends.

They were all silent and David realised that they were all centring their energies on the form of Gerein who was ahead of them, like filings drawn by a magnet they followed in his wake. They had lost any hesitancy based on mistrust. They knew that this was the man who would take them safely into the unknown.

David had lost all his misgivings. He felt safe, certain that all would be well, and felt strong in his own self-confidence.

Then a small dot of light at the end of their vision gradually grew larger. David wondered for a moment if it would recede away from them as they moved forward, like a rainbow, with its unreachable pot of gold, stands just out of reach. It did not recede. The dot of light grew larger and brighter.

Then they were looking down from craggy, eagle dizzy

heights into a green, moist valley where there was the run of water, the glint of light reflecting in spray. Spectrum-coloured lights shot from one side of the valley to the other, like a many prismed, coloured mirror or a cut glass, many faceted crystal stopper to a decanter which he had held to his eye in the sunlight as a child and seen the colours of the rainbow. He remembered vividly the magic he had felt.

They stood awe struck with wonder at the fairy tale beauty of the scene before them.

"It is the Plain of Sol," said Gerein. "We have reached the Plain of Sol."

A look of peace reflected on their faces, as they stood high up on the side of the valley.

"We must rest," said Damian, "before we go any further."

"There is no time," said Gerein. "We must drive ahead to meet up with Scan. We cannot waste time."

They moved ahead with rebelling muscles contracting in their legs, forcing themselves to keep on walking. But their legs kept on giving way under them. They seemed to be losing the voluntary control over their movements.

"I can go no further," said David. "Leave me here. I will catch up with you when I have rested awhile." He lay flat on the dew-wet grass. "I can go no further."

Gerein posted a guard at the highest point of the valley with orders to report any unusual sight or movement.

"Do not hesitate to call if anything strange occurs."

Then they relaxed prostrate on the ground as though they were dead, and not a movement betrayed that they were there. Nothing stirred in the green, peaceful valley, not even the guard lying asleep on the highest escarpment overlooking the valley. No one noticed the party picking their way down among the boulders on the other side of the slope.

Or the black clouds which were collecting threateningly over the mountains. A clash of thunder awoke David from his sleep and a flash of lightning, followed by the hollow claps of thunder which echoed from one side of the valley to the other and one flash after the other lit up the valley with a bright clarity. There was no break in the ferocity of the storm.

"Where are we?" said one man in frightened, blank bewilderment. "What has happened?" He was still half asleep and not sure where he was.

You could see the fear and bewilderment on their faces, as they looked from one to the other, trying to piece together what had brought them to where they were and for what reason. They were in a state of half sleep and shock at the sudden arousal from deep sleep into black darkness intercepted by a bombardment of noise and light.

David said, "It's like wartime when the artillery pounded the enemy lines with shells and people got disturbed by the constant noise."

"It's no more than a bad thunderstorm," said Gerein. "Worst I have ever seen, I must admit."

"The cold is getting into my limbs and the night is dark and fearful."

"There is nothing to fear. You are safe."

"It reminds me of Halloween which we used to celebrate with masks and pumpkins hollowed out in the shape of a face with a candle in them to frighten away the spirits. The night feels like it did then, all spooky and alive with strange shapes and sounds."

"You're not frightened of spirits are you?"

"No! Of course not," said David with a too vehement response to credit that what he had said was true. He couldn't admit to that. They would think he was weak.

"There's no need to fear what you do not understand, David boy. There is more to wonder at in the universe than our eyes can perceive. If you feel an emotion share it, bring it to the surface and do not thrust it deep down inside yourself and deny its existence."

"I was a bit frightened," he said in a half-hearted, shamefaced type of way.

The thunder crashed and crescendoed overhead. The lightning revealed a strange sight. The scuttling forms of unidentifiable shapes forcing their way down the side of the valley.

"They flee like before fire," said Damian. "I fear we have rested too long. We should not have delayed. By now we should have joined forces with Scan." He hesitated and looked around him. "There is a driving together of opposing forces. I sense that is what is happening. Xylo is reaching out, throwing out threads of darkness that are infiltrating the light. We should have made more rapid progress before darkness overwhelmed us with its power. It is the meeting of darkness and light. There will be no turning back now. Evil has to be overcome if we want to retain a vestige of our existence and to live in peace and at one with our fellow men. We all have to face the challenge and not turn and run."

He looked at the apprehensive faces that were looking at him for some guidance and confirmation of what to do in the face of this threat. They all seemed to know the importance of the occasion and that they had to be brave and fight for right.

"Have faith. Do not fear. It has long been known and has been predicted in the books of wisdom that this was about to happen. Being defensive will not achieve anything. We have to challenge the forces of evil, strong in the knowledge that good and right will prevail and will overcome all that threatens it." He looked across the valley. "See, the Plain of Sol stands out like a jewel of light."

He stood with arms outstretched reaching out towards the light a look of awe and wonder on his face.

"It attracts like and repels, rejects anything which is alien and destructive to its luminosity and harmony." His face radiated peace and love. "Can you not feel the magnetic pull that it has on our being? I feel renewed and strong. My depleted energies have been charged, like a battery which has run down and been re-charged and is ready for action again."

Excitement reflected on his face. "Can you not feel it?"

The lightning flashed and the thunder vibrated and clashed around them. A thunderbolt exploded with a cacophony of sound that echoed from one side of the valley to the other. It made David's eardrums feel uncomfortable and sensitive.

"Let us go ahead while this inner strength and drive motivates us."

A tree in front of them split in two as a flash of lightning cut into it and it smouldered like a signal beacon.

"Never fear. Ignore the terrors that surround you. The shrieks and cries you hear are illusion. It sounds as though people are in distress. The sounds are meant to detain you, retard your progress, stop you from going forward." He stood rapt and still.

David followed to where his attention was focussed. The intensity of what he felt reflected on his face in a bright, golden light.

"Watch Sol. Home in on its beacon. It will guide you from all temptations and evil."

A ball of light fell ahead of them and set the vegetation on fire. The flames soared up into the black sky, red and angry, an aura of rage that encircled them with flame.

"Have no fear. We are safe."

Silence greeted these words.

"There is no way out. The fire is all around us. We are cut off."

"Take heart," said Gerein. "Walk straight ahead and see what happens."

They walked forward with fear in their hearts. The flames seemed to be intensifying, thrusting out hungry tongues of fire that lurched towards them singeing their clothes. Sparks showered down on them and the smoke was acrid and made them cough and splutter.

"Keep on walking," said Gerein. "Do not falter."

Then a strange thing happened. As they drew closer to the flames, so close that the flames licked at their faces and each one of them registered that their time was up, that they weren't going to get out of this situation alive, the fire receded, drew back like a curtain being opened so that they were able to pass through to the other side, unhurt and unharmed. The flames drew away from them; its power muted, then flickered and went out.

It ignited again in a defiant flurry of flame and then spluttered into dense, acrid smoke.

This created a fresh spasm of fear.

"We can no longer see the Plain of Sol. It is blotted from our sight. We will lose direction. We will get lost."

A new terror took sway in their hearts.

"The sight you have seen lives on in your memory. You cannot lose that vision of good. Its pull will lead and direct you, you cannot lose what you have already found and made part of what you are. Follow me," said Gerein.

"Rubbish. How do you know any more than we do?" said one rebellious voice. A chorus of agreement sided with what had been said.

"We are lost and without direction."

"Have faith and know that all will be well," said Gerein. "We have passed through many difficulties and we are still together. Do not let evil sway your thoughts and split and divide our solidarity. We have proved strong and unified in the face of all that has happened. Let us stay that way."

Gerein plodded on ahead of them, taking a calculated risk that they would follow. The glow around his slim body was like an enlarged halo of light. It reminded David of the pictures of saints from medieval times, only the light was not just around the head but also right around his body.

Then came a noise which sounded like a thousand million people in intense agony, moaning, groaning, sobbing, begging forgiveness, crying out in the darkness for help, for someone to go to their aid, to pull them from the place in which they had fallen. Voices crying out piteously for help, time and time again, pleading and begging for a gentle word, a kind hand. It was like a Breugel's painting of tormented souls in agony and distress.

"Free us from this mental and physical agony."

"Have pity on us."

"Do not turn your back on our suffering."

"Do not leave us alone with our torment."

Their pleas tore at David with an acuteness that made him feel lacerated inside by their torment and distress.

"Do not listen. Harden your hearts," said Gerein. "Follow my light. They will get the peace they desire when good is restored to full power in the universe. We have a commitment, a duty to reach the Plain of Sol. All that is influenced by good is making in that direction. The more that reach this centre of truth, the greater the power for good. Come. Hesitate no longer. There is no time to lose."

David knew how to close his ears and his mind to the cries of need. He had to harden his heart, distract his attention. He started to sing the well-known refrain

'Lloyd George knows my father.

Father knows Lloyd George' and then

'One man went to mow went to mow a meadow.

One man went to mow went to mow a meadow.

One man and his dog went to mow a meadow.'

These well-known favourites flowed freely from his tongue and blocked out the voices that called out to him from all sides. And the other people with him picked up the tune and joined in enthusiastically centring their attention on what they were singing.

He felt insulated from the external noise and almost forgot that it existed and then he realised that there were no voices. They had stopped. It was quiet, too quiet.

"Now what's happening?" said Damian. "Just when I'd got accustomed to the barrage of noise it stops."

"It's switched down volume," said David cheerfully.

"It's quite a relief," said another man. "I can hear myself think now."

Then the baying of wolves shattered the silence. Howling in an endless crescendo of sound. Shapes and movement slunk among the trees and grass.

Then the sound of fighting, snarling and growling. The sight of them tearing something apart. Tearing pieces from each other in savage greed.

Then they stood with their heads in the air, their muzzles directed upwards to the clear, yellow moon which came out from behind the leaden clouds, and they howled in a way which turned the blood of those who were listening into iced water. The sound made them shudder involuntarily. They were filled with apprehension and fear.

And then the second moon showed itself from behind the clouds. And David noticed that the two moons were moving closer together. There was less distance separating them. The people standing in the open knew instinctively that speed was imperative. They knew that they had to get to the Plain of Sol and be prepared for what was about to happen.

Then the wolves were tearing down the hillside towards them.

"Do not run," said Gerein. "Stand your ground."

Then in front of them was a large, black bear that stood blocking their way. He grunted angrily and looked at them with small, malevolent, pig-like eyes. Then he charged towards them. Their numbers split as the party divided to get out of the way.

"Stay together," said Gerein. "Do not allow him to drive a wedge between us." He advanced towards the bear threateningly and it retreated, turned tail and slunk away without a backward glance.

"What did I say?" said Gerein. "Good is with us. Have no fear. Stand your ground."

He swung around abruptly in response to the snarling of wolves. They growled in an aggressive, threatening, attacking manner, ringing in around them and then retreating, drawing back. Then back in with bared teeth. The smell of wolf was heavy in the air. Their hot breath misted the air and saliva trickled from their slobbering muzzles and dripped down on the soil.

They turned from Gerein's threatening rush and ran back among the bushes where their red eyes glowed in the dark. Then the number of eyes grew fewer and fewer and then they were gone. The men relaxed as the danger disappeared.

The atmosphere changed and once again they could see the Plain of Sol within their sight. Its light arced out towards them, holding them in its extended beam and its radiancy gave them hope and encouragement.

25

Scan felt expansive with gratitude. Emma was alive and well. The delight which radiated like a light shone from his face, reflected in his eyes. He hugged her to him.

"I don't want to let you go just in case you'll disappear from my sight like a mirage." He looked at her. "You are real. You are Emma, dear little Emma." He looked at her again. "I have missed you so much, it fills me with delight to see you in front of me, to know that no harm has come to you."

He stood back for a short time and looked with great love at her and then he embraced her tenderly and gently. She felt comfortable close to him.

"In a short space of time you have become part of my life as though we have always known each other and never been apart. When you disappeared I was filled with anguish and grief, as though I had lost a loved part of myself." He looked long and hard at her. "You were safe and protected all the time." His face reflected great tenderness and joy. "My fears for your safety were unfounded." He laughed with the sheer joy of the occasion.

"And where is David?" said Emma.

There was silence between them for a moment. A look of sadness passed across Emma's face and her eyes filled with tears. "I fear the worst. The expression on your face tells it all. Tell me! Tell me what you know." She hesitated for a moment as though she could not get the words out. "Is he dead?"

"Let me put you in the picture. I do not know what has

happened to David. It may well be that he is all right and that we will meet up again with him in time. He was with us until we passed through the country of the Sea Witch. One minute he was there and the next he had disappeared. We hunted high and low, on mountain and plain, in wood and field but he was nowhere to be found." There was a break in the conversation and then Scan sighed deeply. "We should have known better than to rest where the Sea Witch has dominion. She has devious ways of making people her own. She catches you with pictures of things that you want or would enjoy. She makes them so real that she can lure you from reality into the world of fantasy. You leave your friends and those you hold dear and follow some fantasy that she feeds into your mind.

"She is cunning and clever. She intuitively knows what thoughts and desires are uppermost in your mind. She can tune in to the thoughts of the person she has decided to make her own. There is little chance of escape once she has made the decision that you are to be hers."

Emma shuddered. She felt cold with misery. Would they meet up with David again or had she seen him for the last time? She felt sick with anguish. It could not be. It had never occurred even in her wildest dreams that anything could happen to David. There were times when, in anger, she had wished that he would go from her life, and the memory of those thoughts sat heavily on her conscience now. She felt guilty and tormented by the possibility that she had been at the root of his disappearance. In some magic way, what she had been thinking might have had an effect and had caused some harm to happen to her brother.

Then, he wasn't the type of person to be affected by what other people said, never mind what they thought. She had always envied him his detachment. Their moods did not seem to have any effect on the way he felt or acted. He was in his little world, insulated against feedback or other people's reactions. Some would say he was insensitive.

Whatever it was, it left his central core of confidence untouched and he retained his belief in himself.

Emma often wished she could be the same but she was just the opposite, fiery and quick-tempered. She had learnt to bait him, to make David's hackles rise, but it was a learnt response to observing what made him tick. She had found his Achilles heel and knew where he was vulnerable. 'That's it', thought Emma. 'Everybody has their weak, soft under parts which are vulnerable and easily hurt and damaged'.

"Perhaps he'll be all right," she said hopefully to Scan, trying to absolve herself from guilt at the implication that she may have been involved in some way in his disappearance.

They sat down on the sorrel scented grass and Emma told Scan about her bid to bring Kyoto to safety and how, at the last moment, she had lost him. The haul across the white wilderness of snow and the path of fallen insects that she had followed and Scan laughed.

"I remember seeing those."

They exchanged stories about the adventures they had experienced when they were apart. They felt close and finely tuned to each other. Then there was a flash of golden light. The gold of daffodils in full flower in the month of March, breaking the hold of winter with their cheery, energising beauty. The colour became transparent and then crystal clear, as spring water. It bubbled across her vision. It continually changed from opaque, cloudy, to translucent to clear. She had never experienced anything like it before.

She tried to ignore the intrusion of this pulsating golden light, but it would not be ignored.

"What is worrying you?" said Scan with obvious concern.

"It's nothing," said Emma hesitantly. "Nothing."

"But there is something distressing you."

"It's nothing really, nothing," she repeated, but

inwardly she felt disturbed. She was only half attentive to what Scan was saying; her attention was focused on the subliminal character of her thoughts. She did not understand what was going on.

"Tell me," said Scan. "There may be some significance in what is happening." There was silence for a moment or so and then he continued. "There is something bothering you. At a quick guess, I think I am getting a similar experience, like breaks in circuitry. I was talking to you about Kyoto and my mind went blank and I could not remember what I had been talking about. And you stopped in mid sentence as though something was distracting you." He stopped waiting to hear what she had to say. "I have been getting this bright golden light, potentilla to amber, one minute cloudy, the next minute translucent and when it cleared and became as transparent as glass, there was a scene, a picture which I could not quite make out and the harder I tried the more indefinite and hazy it became."

"That's exactly what is happening to me," said Emma with a sigh of relief. "At least it is a shared experience."

"Why didn't you say something? There must be some explanation for what is happening." He stroked his chin thoughtfully and his brow furrowed as though deep in thought. "If I could make out what is in the picture then perhaps we would have a clearer idea of what is going on."

Emma bit her under lip as though deep in thought. "I found it quite disturbing. The intrusion was strong enough to interrupt my stream of thought and then I lost touch with where I left off in the conversation I was having with you. It was a struggle to focus my attention back and take in what you were saying. Terribly rude, I know." She laughed.

"I think we ought to focus inward on this picture at the same time. Tune in on the same wavelength."

The two moons in the sky hung on the horizon. Stillness was suspended in the air like a thread of gossamer from a spider's spinnerets. Emma and Scan sat side by side in the green, dew-covered, sorrel grass but nothing happened. It had all disappeared. There was nothing forthcoming.

"Well, we've done our best. Sometimes the association becomes clearer at a later date and then the gaps in the picture are filled in and everything becomes clear. It's best not to rush things."

He reverted back to the time that they had travelled apart. "You say you followed the skein of fallen insects which led like a path in the direction that we had taken. It was as though you were under divine protection."

Then Emma said, "The same thing happened when those horrid winged creatures with the smell of corruption and death caught up with us. If you remember, our party split up."

"How can I ever forget!" said Scan.

"I was helped at that time in an unbelievable way."

"Tell me more," said Scan looking thoughtfully at Emma. "When we did go back after the terrifying creatures of Xylo were thought to have left, there was no sign of you. All that remained were the dead, not a living creature. It sickened me to see torn bodies lying in the trammelled grass. Terrible injuries inflicted on them."

Emma visibly blanched as the words brought back memories that had been consigned to her unconscious. The screams of terror from the injured as the infuriated creatures attacked time and time again until there were no further cries or moans. The only sound was the raucous cries of crows as they circled around and around before settling on the ground where the massacre had occurred.

Emma remembered the way the pterodactyl-sized bats swooped down with exposed, grimacing teeth from which the soft mouthparts were retracted and sinking their talons and teeth into the unprotected bodies of the people they were attacking. It was horrendous and she shivered involuntarily at the thought.

"They protected me, you know, shielded me from sight. If that hadn't happened you would have found me among the slain."

"What protected you?" asked Scan.

"You'll only laugh and tell me it was imagination."

"Well, give me a chance!"

"It was the blackberry brambles. There, I knew you'd find it amusing," said Emma peevishly.

Scan wondered if a hint of a smile had appeared on his face. It was just possible. It was the way Emma came out with it as though she expected a denial and opposition. Her words came out in an explosive, defiant challenge, as though she dared anybody to query what she knew had happened.

"Stranger things than that have occurred. There may be no logical explanation. Nature is feeling and works in its own way to bring good into the universe."

"They somehow moved over me. No! I didn't roll under them. I know I didn't! They seemed to be whispering words of encouragement. They told me to keep still and not to move otherwise I would give away where I was. They spoke in a melodic tone like the whispering of wind in the treetops, even the sound was soothing and comforting. They scratched me with their thorns but to this day I am sure they told me to keep still as I was in fearsome danger. No, I wasn't having hallucinations! It's no good looking at me like that," said Emma defensively.

"I'm not decrying what you have said. We cannot understand all things." He hesitated for a brief spell. "Every single object, life form has a divine potential and purpose and can be influenced to help in the cause of good."

"After what has happened, I will never be the same person again. If I do go back to my old world I wonder if they will be able to accept the new me. There is nothing haphazard about life. There is purpose and meaning, of that I am sure. We all have a part, a place to play in it, like each geological fragment goes into a conglomerate to form a whole. I no longer feel like a leaf blown along the ground."

"Quietly!" said Scan. "Something moved in that clump of bushes. I saw a movement from the corner of my eye."

"Where?" said Emma apprehensively.

"Do not look now. I want whatever it is to think we have not seen it, that it is unobserved. Do not look in the direction I mentioned. Go on talking normally, as though nothing has happened."

"What has happened?" said Emma.

"Shush! Not too loudly. I'd like to know what is out there lurking in the undergrowth."

"You imagined it," said Emma in a disgruntled way. Just when she was getting philosophical. "I tell you there is nothing there," and she turned in the direction where Scan had noticed the movement. "I was wrong, there is something there." She stopped in mid sentence. "I saw a movement, so quickly at first that I thought I had imagined it. It was so rapid and insubstantial."

"We're obviously being observed," said Scan. He watched the movement in the bushes from the corner of his eye. "Do not let them know that we have noticed anything," he whispered to Emma. "Be ready to defend yourself but do not attack even if you are provoked. We are basically peace loving people."

"That movement is still there," said Emma impatiently.

"I'm going to walk towards the bushes and make whatever it is come out into the open." He turned toward the thick scrub and disappeared among the undergrowth.

Emma felt apprehensive and exposed. She hoped no harm would come to him. She unashamedly loved Scan.

"He'll be all right," said a voice behind her.

There was a movement in the bushes and then to Emma's surprise, a well known figure came across the clearing to where they were standing with Scan behind him, a cheerful look on both their faces. She ran forward to greet the man in front of her but as she drew nearer to him, he disintegrated like mist before the wind.

She drew back not sure what to make of the situation. She felt confused and she looked at Scan's face for reassurance.

"Thought forms," he said.

"Thought forms?" she repeated after him. "Thought forms?"

"They come from the subconscious. They can be a very powerful deterrent when used with discrimination. We all dream at night. Sometimes these are soothing and pleasant, other times frightening and even terrifying."

The baying of wolves and the high pitched yapping and howling in the darkness made Emma shudder. She drew nearer to Scan. He drew back suddenly from her and then, realising what was happening, relaxed and spoke to her comfortingly. "It's all right Emma," and added, as though by way of explanation, "You know I was telling you about thought forms. We all think in pictures and shapes. I suspect the power of Xylo is trying to exert control over us. As you came closer I did not see you. The Sea Witch was standing where you are now standing, water rippling all around her and her hypnotic eyes were drawing me out of myself and I was being drowned, drawn under the depths of the ocean. I felt sea water lapping, pulling at my mind, dragging me under." Scan's eyes became dreamy and distant.

A look of horror came over Emma's face and she shrieked out loud "Don't come near me. Get away!" And she pulled as far as she could away from where Scan was standing. She looked fearfully at the patterned back of a snake as it slithered in a zigzag movement towards her. Its lizard like tongue protruded in and out. She felt paralysed with fear, unable to move. Her muscles refused to react; her movement was frozen. When she screamed and cried out for help there was no sound from her vocal chords, just an abbreviated squeak that only seemed audible to her. The scream, which was on her lips, was frozen in time, in an instant of mockery.

Scan realised what was happening. "Listen to me," he said. "It is not real, it is an illusion. It comes from the recesses of your mind. Snap your fingers. Break the spell. It is you and what you fear. Recognise what is happening."

She heard Scan's voice at a distance. She was still mesmerised by the scarlet-backed snake, which was moving towards her. It was getting closer and closer and there was nothing she could do. And then it came into her mind. 'Snap your fingers. Break the spell. It is all in the mind. It is not real' and she felt herself coming around as from a spell and Scan was standing in front of her with a look of great love on his face and she felt drawn and lost in that love.

He momentarily held her close and he noticed the rapid beating of her heart, the warmth of her body. He waited patiently for her to recover her calmness and for her heartbeat to return to its normal rate.

Eventually she pulled gently away. A look of gratitude on her face and her eyes radiated warmth and love.

"The Wizard of Xylo knows what he is doing. He holds us up, delays us when time is imperative. We must make for the Plain of Sol, there is no time to lose."

He strode ahead and she followed in his footsteps.

The yellow beam of light that insistently seemed to be invading her thought processes was once again disturbing Emma. It became more and more insistent. Above her in the dark sky the two moons moved closer and closer together. It must have some significance.

Emma wondered if Scan was having the same experience. It had happened before to the two of them. Was there something trying to let her know of some danger, tell her something important? What could it mean?

It was insistent. It could not be denied. She tried to maintain a stillness and quiet within her. Attentive, calm and listening.

And then the yellow light gave way to a picture, thumb-sized, minute, but in fine detail. It was like a transparency. Nothing was left out.

There was something in the picture towards which her attention was being drawn, underground seams of oxide and yellow ore and crystals that glinted with a light of their own. Stalagmites hung down in a curtain from which water dripped incessantly and mounting up from the floor and almost joining the fringe above a replica formation of icicles glistened in the eerie, underground light. The light was emitted by the crystal formations that shone with an energy of their own.

In the cave were beautiful works of art, golden bowls, cups, plates, tureens and vases. All finely engraved. And then she saw Scan being presented with something by a small, elfin man. It was a large, shield-like object that was almost too beautiful to describe. In the floor of the object was a yellow stone that radiated light like the sun. Iridescent, like the wings of a dragonfly which flicked and scintillated picking up rainbow colours, colours which Emma had never realised existed, delicate and poignant, bringing temporarily into focus every gradient and spectrum of light. It lent an indescribable beauty to what she was seeing.

Emma knew intuitively that her attention was being drawn to the gemstone for a reason, that it had some association with what was about to happen. And then the beauty of the object zoomed in towards her as though it was being caught in a gigantic lens that was magnifying it in detail. She was looking through the crystal. She felt its innate power and strength. It acted as a focal point for energy.

Then she saw the two moons in the sky converging together, getting closer and closer, until they were touching each other, rim to rim. Then they moved over each other, like two ten pence pieces superimposed one upon the other.

They had merged and were one.

And their light and power intensified and a beam like a laser shaft of light focussed on the yellow stone.

Emma knew that the earth forces were being balanced and she was seeing a preview of what was about to happen on the Plain of Sol. It would happen if the circumstances were right and enough people reached the radiant centre of light. Emma saw the energy from the circle of light around the stone activate the other crystals in the soil, and the light that it produced was healing and nurturing and warm with a build up of vibrating energy.

There must be some reason in what was happening.

She followed Scan's purposeful figure and she listened attentively to what he was saying.

"I am getting those pictures again. I can see a ring of stones, like the megaliths, which stand on Stonehenge. The two moons are edging closer to each other. The dial in the middle stone registers the movement of shadow. Time is short. If we fail to reach the circle by the zenith of the moon, another year will be spent in the darkness and the power of Xylo will extend still further into what remains of Thanbodia." His eyes glazed and distanced for the moment as though he was part of the future and then he went on. "The Plain of Sol stands out like a beacon, flashing encouragement to those who are receptive to its vibration. Its magnetic pull is drawing us towards its healing centre. A core of power, of good. We have the law of the above and below on our side." Again that far off look appeared in his eyes. "We are all compounded of good, are good." That dreamy look again. "It is only our negativity which gets in the way but indirectly it is this very negativity which helps us to grow and to use the difficulties in our lives constructively." Again that far off look appeared in his eyes.

"We must keep the light from the Plain of Sol in front of us," said Emma. "Link that inner part of us to it, and like the guidance of the North Star, it will lead us where we are meant to go."

"You speak with wisdom," said Scan with humility.

"Where are the others?" said Emma. "For a moment I had forgotten their existence."

As the words left her mouth it was as though a partition fell away from in front of them revealing the rest of the party.

"There you are!" said a relieved voice. "Somehow we got separated. Cut off by a dense fog that made us lose our sense of direction. We had no idea which way to go. We have been wandering around aimlessly trying to find our bearings, until we made a group decision to stay where we were until the mist lifted."

"You did the right thing," said Scan. "But," he added in a deliberate, meaningful way as though he wanted to get a point across, "if you had taken a deep breath and blown it out in a steady stream, the mist would have lifted like a veil pulled back from your face."

As they drew nearer to the Plain of Sol they felt peace and warmth radiating out towards them with stronger and a more intense energy. A look of calm and tranquillity came over Scan's face and the glow intensified around him. Emma noticed the same peaceful expression on the faces of the people who were with them and within herself she felt an inrush, a boost of peace, confidence and love.

"All will be well," said Scan. "Of this, I am sure. We will reach the ring of stones before the zenith is over."

Even as these words were said the light seemed to recede from around them. The sky was darkening. The growl of thunder echoed through the hills with an eerie resonance. The clap bounced off one side of the valley and back to the other, from one overhang to the other.

But in the middle of the darkness the Plain of Sol stood out like a jewel of light. Like a lighthouse, it signalled a warning to the realm of darkness and a beacon of hope to those who were receptive to the light.

"It is numbers we need," said Scan, "to make the ring of light."

"I do not understand," said Emma peevishly. "You are always talking in riddles."

"You will understand," said Scan. "All will become clear to you when the time is right. Life is like a voyage of discovery, movement and change. One step is taken at a time. Then a little more is revealed. Another piece of jigsaw fits into the pattern of your growth. Be patient, little one. It will all become clear to you when the time is right."

"There is one thing you seem to have forgotten," said Emma in a peevish, spoilt way. "The bell and Tingate Well. That is part of the prophecy."

"All will be revealed. All will be revealed. The sequence of events is underway. Just like the circles that arc out when a pebble is thrown into a pond. Nothing will stop what has already been put into action. It will move on to completion. We need to be in the right place at the right time." He hesitated. "Then all will be well."

Then they heard the movements of twigs snapping underfoot.

"Someone else approaches," said Scan.

And they stood in the clearing looking apprehensively in the direction from which the noise had come. Then the shapes of people keeping together in a group, not strung out singly in Indian file but huddled together as though fearful of getting unstuck if they moved too far from each, other came into view.

"Welcome," said Scan. "Welcome."

There was silence, then the signs of recognition as though it was too unbelievable to sink in at first.

"Is it you Scan?" And Gerein and David stood in front of them.

Gerein threw his arms around Scan and David hugged Emma to him, and then stood back as though to make sure that it was really Emma, and then embraced her hungrily.

"I thought we would never meet again. It is so good to see you."

They eyed each other with eager, affectionate glances of delight.

"I cannot fully tell you the joy and delight I feel," said Scan. "We are together again to take place in the battle between darkness and light. I can tell you that on the Plain of Sol there is a circle of stones that has been built in the past over a strong energy source from the earth. The circle is made of uprights and lintels and central to these cromlechs and standing stones is a large central slab that centralises the earth energies to a point. It has a circular hole cut into the middle and radial lines cut out like a sunburst, in ray formation. It is here where the final battle will be fought."

Emma looked miserable. "Will there be much slaughter and death? I fear war with its suffering and loss. The sadness of a child without a father, wife without husband and the innocent caught in the violence and death." Pictures of the result of war and devastation flashed through Emma's mind. The starved, the marasmic, haunted with what they had experienced. Their unnaturally large eyes dulled with apathy, full of pain, old, worldly wise beyond their time, naivety and innocence blanked out by what they had endured. Suffering stamped on their features. Their bodies without any subcutaneous fat, skin taut, drawn tight across bones where each bulge and joint stood out starkly with thinning of the skin over the surface.

"This can't happen. I have just got David back." She threw her arms around him and clung to him hungrily. "If I were to lose you again I don't know what I'd do. I could not endure the pain. Please take care." She sobbed emotionally and tears ran unchecked down her cheeks. "I want peace. To be with the people that I am fond of." She turned to David. "To get used of having you around again."

"That's a record for the book. If I'd heard it from someone else instead of being here on the spot I would not have believed it." He moved away from her clinging hands as though her display of emotion was making him feel uncomfortable and ill at ease. "You have certainly changed. This is not the same Emma I used to know. I'll only believe it is a reality when you act in the same way when we're back home with Mum and Dad."

That did it! The memory of home, in Emma's frail state, drew on an inner need and she started to cry filled with nostalgia and a surge of memories.

"Do you think we'll ever see Mum and Dad again or have we been away so long that things will have changed beyond recognition?" She looked at David hoping to see some signs of understanding but he was impassive and distant. "It is so lonely to have feelings which you cannot share with someone else, to experience them all alone."

David looked uncomfortably at her. "I do understand but I wish you'd belt up. I hate emotional scenes. Everybody is looking at you."

"I don't care. Why should I care? You've provoked enough emotional scenes in your time. This is how I feel at this present moment. I'm tired of not acknowledging how I feel," and she added, "I don't care if the whole world is watching." There was silence for a moment between them. Then Emma said, "I want Mum and Dad." She hesitated for a moment. "When did I last have a bath? When did I last wash my hair?"

"It's all right. She must be feeling better; she's worried about how she looks. It's water she needs to unlayer the dirt."

The tears left white channels down her grubby cheeks.

"You can see she hasn't seen water for days Scan. Let her bathe and she'll be her old self again."

Scan put a comforting arm around Emma's shoulders. The stress and strain that she had gone through had come to a level where it could no longer simmer but had to have some outlet. He drew her tenderly towards him.

"All will be well," and he ran his fingers gently across her brow. She felt the imprint of them even when they were no longer touching her forehead. They brought that well known feeling of calmness that spread in warm waves around her body. Her breathing steadied and the sobbing eased back.

Scan held her for a short time. Then he said, "Darkness is drawing closer. Even though it is midday, the darkness of night is overwhelming us. I fear for our safety if more do not come to form the ring."

"The ring?" said David in a mystified manner. "What do you mean? The ring? Doesn't make sense to me."

"You'll see," said Scan. "The time is not yet right to reveal the secret of the ring. It is age old. Passed down from one generation to another in the secret induction. When the boy reaches the age of wisdom he has to be initiated into the secret, so that when the time is right they will lead and know what to do. It is part of our culture."

"All boys?" said Emma. "What about the girls?"

"It is minority of families and no girls," he said with a half smile on his face. "Perhaps that will come in time. It's rather like the Knights of the Round Table. The oldest surviving families of the land."

"It's so dark I can't see my hand in front of my face. I'm frightened. My teeth are clattering together like china pots, and my legs are shaking as though they are going to give way underneath me."

"It's all right, little one. There are more people coming to support us."

"More to follow too," said another man. "They are flooding from the valleys and hills where they have been hiding, waiting for the call, the rally to join forces and to make the ring."

"Once more this talk of the circle. Can't you explain the significance of the words?"

"There is a time and a place for all things. A time for

waiting. A time for movement. A time for knowing and a time for ignorance of that knowledge. A time for closeness. A time for separation. Be of good cheer, it will become clear when the time is right."

Emma felt Scan had the makings of a priest within him or whatever holy man was in charge of the spiritual care of the people of Thanbodia. There was something in him of substance and with spiritual direction. It made her feel safe and secure, warm and comfortable.

"I understand," she answered. "It is well with me."

"That is good, good," said Scan

But Emma was indifferent to his words. She felt better. The fear that had stiffened her muscles into rigidity and made her heart bounce and pound in her chest had eased. She felt positive and relaxed. Somehow, Scan always had this effect on her. All would be well of that she was sure.

More and more people poured down the hillside and flooded on to the Plain of Sol.

A strange thing seemed to be happening, the aura of light was extending outward, taking back some of the darkness. Tendril-like fingers inching, arcing into the surrounding countryside. And the light shone around Scan's face with a luminosity that made his features seem insubstantial and unreal, as though he was not of this world.

And Emma wondered at it. But even as the wonder awoke in her a deep sense of peace, a wave of energy, of power blanketed her off from the people she had been with. She was alone.

"Scan, Scan," pleaded Emma, but her words were carried away by the thunder of noise that was closing in around her, effectively cutting her off from everyone else.

A cacophony of hate lashed and shredded through her. Emma knew there was something she had to do. The separation had happened with reason. She knew instinctively that she had to find Tingate Well. The knowledge burned inside her with certainty and force. It gave impetus to her tired body and mind. It still craved comfort and quiet, but she knew there would be time for that later on. Now, she had work to do. She had been moved involuntarily from the radiancy of the light around Scan into the impenetrable darkness.

It hit her like a brick wall, the impact of a car against a solid object when it collided at great speed. But Emma found she was protected. A rubber-like shell resisted, spread out the shock waves, and absorbed them as the bumps are evened out by the shock absorbers in a car when the road is cratered and uneven.

Within her heart she knew she was protected and safe, that no harm would come to her. Her loneliness was of the body not the spirit. She felt resolution within her. It reflected in the set of her chin, the steadiness of her eyes. The way they seemed to look beyond the present into the future. Once more the past, present and the future were a firm, solid line and she was part of it.

She knew that they were waiting for her on the Plain of Sol. Waiting for her to accomplish the prophecy that had been written in the sacred book of Thanbodia. And the resolution mounted inside her with certainty. She knew what to do. Emma had no need for instruction. It was written within each cell, each molecule of her living body.

Her destiny was to complete, to bring together the last pieces of the jigsaw puzzle, the pieces that would complete the overthrowing of the forces of darkness. But darkness did not see defeat in the resolute light of her face. Did not need to run from the light that radiated from around her. It tore at the outer, auric shell, hammering with a derisive, blistering force at the protective shell that surrounded her. It tried to eat, to bore into the density of its protection. Even a minuscule hole would drain the protection from around her, as an egg can be blown by a pinhole at each end of the shell.

But the attack was of no avail. Her strength withstood all the frontal attacks, showed no weakness to the hostility and evil quailed and quaked before her innocence. But craft and guile are the kindred brothers of the forces of darkness and they knew how to turn all situations to their advantage. Would the plan they had work?

With an intuitive knowledge they knew that they could direct all their negativity and greyness and darkness at Emma. They saw weaknesses in the youth, the innocence, the lack of sophistication and experience.

She did not realise of what they were capable. And they laughed and cackled to themselves. Get her to work with us instead of against us. Get at her from within. They formulated a thought form of Scan.

He was there by her side. The warmth of his eyes holding her safe and secure. It stilled the buffeting, made light break through darkness and revealed the physical features of what lay ahead of her.

She knew that her destination was to reach Tingate Well. Could this be Tingate Well? It was possible. She had never seen it before. It was an octagonal building constructed from wrought ironwork. There were stairs leading up to a circular, stone-flagged platform from each side of the eight-sided faceting. In the middle was a fountain, with a drinking cup anchored by a metal chain. Above, a canopy of intricate decorative wrought iron that centred to a point upon which a weathercock moved directionally in the wind.

Emma mentally took in what was before her, trying to make sense and connect her thoughts together. She was sure she had to go up the steps and lift the cup from the fountain and fill the cup with the crystal clear water that jetted up into the air. Scan was with her and she knew that there was no danger when he was by her side. She looked up at the ornate, roofed grill, which rose to a sectionalised point.

Then Scan was gone, no longer with her. He had disappeared without a word of explanation.

The darkness descended whip like upon her. It

obscured all vision. Emma caught her breath in fear and screamed out loud. Her voice sounded strangled and thin as though it was not part of her.

Even as she registered these feelings of fear, she felt the scoring scratch of something sharp against her arm and looking down she could see only darkness before her, but there was a sticky substance under her fingers as she felt her arm.

Could it be blood? Panic welled up in her. Where was Scan? He'd been there only a moment ago. Why had he left her?

Then a still voice within her, so quiet as to be almost imperceptible crept into her consciousness.

"You go in this direction at your peril."

'What did it mean?' thought Emma, defensively.

Then Scan was in front of her, motioning her to follow and not to listen to anyone but him.

"Oh! There you are," she said, with an indrawn breath of relief. "I'm so glad to see you."

"All is well. Come with me and do as I say." This was reinforced by a forcible nudge that nearly knocked her off balance. Then she heard the inner voice loud and clear within her "You are in great danger. What you see in front of you is illusion, a figment of the imagination. Close your eyes and be guided by my voice."

"What am I to believe?" said Emma. "My senses are deceiving me. I see a figure which is the double of Scan and he tells me all is well and to follow him and do as he says. It sounds and looks like Scan! What am I to think?" She put her finger to her lip pensively. "And then there is this voice and what does it say? Block out what is before you, you are being influenced by forces beyond your control, that aim to take control of your will and deflect you from what you are meant to do. What am I to believe? What am I to do?"

Again that inner voice, persistent and persuasive. "Take care! Listen only to what I say. They have made a thought

211

form, identical to me in all ways and they have projected it in front of you. It is not the Scan you know. Do not make any plans or follow any directions or information which you get from that source."

"Give me some proof, some evidence, please!" pleaded Emma totally immersed in the internal dialogue with Scan. "I do not know what to believe, what to do," she hesitated. "I am so confused by it all."

She gave a fleeting glance at the figure of Scan in front of her and firmly closed her eyes and directed all her attention away from the outside. As though by magic when she opened her eyes after two or three minutes of intense concentration, the external figure of Scan had gone, disappeared like mist before the wind. In front of her was an open stretch of grassland, bounded by coppice trees of mountain ash, hazel, sloe and bramble.

"Go straight ahead," said the voice. "You have done well. You have passed the test. Over the brow of the hill is an escarpment. Go along the ridge of rock and down into the valley. The valley is wooded. Have no fear. Continue on the path that leads to the floor of the valley. You will come to a clearing bounded by grey, smooth barked trees. These beech trees are the seven daughters of wisdom. They point to Tingate Well."

Emma felt as though positive action was influencing everything that she did. There was no cause for fear and notes of gentle, soft healing music flitted like a backdrop through her mind. It gave her a sense of centring and stability that made firm every footstep that she took. She walked forward through the coppice to the base of the valley. Before her was the compass point which she'd been looking out for.

She counted the grey trunked boles of the beech trees that towered skyward in an interwoven trellis of branches and leaves. The seven daughters of wisdom.

"One, two, three, four, five, six, seven." They arrowed

towards a narrow path that snaked downward into a tunnel of foliage. The pathway opened out into a clearing, open to the sky. In front of her was a half circular construction, hollowed in the centre, and on the other side was a similar, mirror-like reflective image. It was built of natural stone, dry stone walled by craftsman.

Was this what she had been sent to find? An overhead bridge of rock, which connected the still depths of the water, joined the two sides and something glittered and shone in the bottom of the pool. It reflected and shone. It caught the light and flashes of patterned colour shimmered across the water.

Emma moved closer to identify the cause of the refracted light. What could be causing such a beautiful effect? It was as though the raindrops had been caught in a prism of light that had created a rainbow effect. It was like the droplets of dew on a cobweb caught in the early morning light and the beauty of it temporarily caught her imagination, and made her catch her breath in wonder and delight.

She bent to pick up the object from the bottom of the water but a restraining hand prevented her from doing it, and a strident voice challenged her with the following words. "How dare you intrude where you are not welcome? You disturb the vibrations of peace with your physical presence. All the forces of destruction will follow wherever you go if you destroy the beauty of its spell."

She moved backwards in response to the sharpness of the words. "I mean no harm. It is beautiful and I wanted to see what it is. I was only going to take it out of the water and examine it. I mean no harm," she repeated. She moved forward again.

"Stand back. Do not come any closer."

"Who is this that challenges my access?" said a strong, purposeful voice, and it took Emma a moment to realise that the words had come from her mouth. "You stand in my way at your peril."

"You dare to challenge the guardians of the well?" said a voice thick with anger and frustrated exasperation. "Go away while you have the chance. Do not provoke me to mischief. You do not realise what dangerous ground you trespass upon. Turn and go before it is too late. Be gone, I say. Do not arouse the anger of the green people."

"Green people... elves and imps." Her output stopped as she listened attentively for what would come next.

'Make yourself known to them', said her internal voice. 'They are the guardians of the well as they have stated. The silver that glitters in front of you has been fashioned by elfin fingers, chased by elfin chisels. They know of your coming. Make known your identity. Tell them who you are.'

Emma drew herself up to her full height in an imposing regal way. "You do not appear to recognise me. I am Emma, and it is foretold that a girl of my name will come to Tingate Well. I have come to get the silver bell." She stopped for a moment. "I am Emma."

At her words she became surrounded by light. It spread out from the well and into the darkness. The resolution inside her became firm and strong but paralleling it was a strange sense of humility. Warmth and affection radiated out from her in an expansive, giving way.

They knew of her and the legend associated with her coming and the green folk became visible and she was surrounded by their silvery laughter. She was no longer a threat.

"We have long awaited your coming. It delights us to welcome you."

A silver bell chased with a pattern of such delicacy that it looked almost too fragile to handle was handed to her with reverence. Even as the tiny clapper vibrated backward and forwards the silver, high-pitched tones rang insistently out into the darkness, which seemed to withdraw and the light was dispersing the shadows. The light was visibly ranging upward and outwards, extending further and further into the distance. And the peace and joy was growing within Emma.

The green folk were dancing a frenzied dance of joy. Feet of green scarcely touching the turf, as the circles spun faster and faster, faster and faster. The movement blurred into one and no single form could be identified. Her hand was taken and she was whirling around to the dance, her feet scarcely touching the ground.

Then her hand was loosed and it was all turned off as though a light bulb had blown, or a light switch had thrown a fuse.

Emma was alone holding the silver bell to her.

It still sent out scintillating sounds that vibrated far, far into the distance.

26

Scan directed the people, who flooded down on to the Plain of Sol to join hands and form a circle, within a circle. Circle, after circle of people stood around the mighty uprights of stone. He instructed them to concentrate, to centre all their energies to exclude evil and darkness and make what was to be done, easier to accomplish.

The solidity of the force around them was almost palpable, almost visible. A substantial energy that seemed to be building up, getting stronger and stronger. Nothing like this had been experienced before. It was mystical in origin, not of this world.

And a scintillating silver sound vibrated in the atmosphere around them. Each person felt the subtle movement and vibration, though they were unaware of the altering in frequency as their physical bodies became lighter and more insubstantial. It was as though their feet were not touching the ground. They were lifting off becoming part of the sky and the air.

They felt part of the moving light and were at one with its purpose. The scintillating, bell-like tone had unplugged the deafened ears of the Thanbodians. The noise, as though amplified by many loudspeakers, thundered in their ears and the shock of it temporarily put them off balance.

The noises seemed to hold all the negative and destructive forces in the universe. The hurricane and the tropical storm, with its continual flashes of lightning and the clash of thunder. The impact of heat and sand from the desert parts of the world. The earth movements of quakes opening out huge, gaping rents and chasms in the ground which had no solidity, and the sea, raging with far flung spray and waves that rode so high that the troughs looked like bottomless depths and the peaks threatened to engulf the ground that they rode toward and swallow it up so that it would no longer exist.

They were aware of this happening like a backdrop. No sooner had this awareness of fear come into their emotional field than it was supplanted by an indescribable ecstasy of joy.

The noise, the fury and the agony did not touch them. It was held at bay. It could not impinge on that central core of strength that their collective power had helped to build.

Scan knew that all the forces of good were assisting them to block, to drive away, to repel darkness and build up the light.

Still darkness struggled and strove to extend its influence. They heard the high pitched whine and shriek of cats and their low, menacing growl and spitting as they attacked with ferocious savagery. The sound cut the darkness. Wings beat noisily above them bringing the threat of attack closer and closer. But the darkness struggled to no avail.

The higher vibratory sound of the bell-like music and the mellow tones of the flute and harp were drawing more and more light down on to the plain. It shone with light brighter than the white light of the Mediterranean or the white heat of the desert. It was so bright that it hurt the eyes and forced the onlooker to, at first, gaze surreptitiously through hand shaded, slitted eyes and then close, shut out the scene completely.

It was brighter than the flash following the explosion of an atomic bomb. So bright that it burnt up all solid within its path and reduced the density of all that it touched.

*   *   *

And from afar, Emma saw what was happening as though videoed to her on a big panoramic viewfinder. It was as though all the vibratory levels were represented on the Plain of Sol that night. All were contributing their part in the scheme of things. Each one was aware of the importance of their contribution, of what they had to give.

There were representatives from deep in the bowels of the earth, to the upper reaches of the sky and the outer universe, all singing praise and joy in this new found light which was making them whole. What was fragmented and dualistic became unified and at one. What was splintered and diseased was healed.

Emma felt this change within herself. She felt a flow of love encompassing her, and surrounding her with its peace, and it built up to overflow point and the energy flowed out from her. It embraced everything. She felt compassion and understanding for all life forms, for all that existed.

All resentment, anger, pain and fear disintegrated like mist before the wind. She wanted to stretch her arms wide and hold the world to her in love. She felt a depth of gratitude that it had happened in her time, and that she had been witness to the beauty of the occasion.

She knew that nothing would be exactly the same after this event. Things would be changed. Attitudes, opinions and viewpoints would be different. Care and understanding would take the place of criticism and judgement. People would not dictate and threaten and tell what to do, but allow people to express their inner self in their own way. Would support, strengthen, give love but not act as judge and jury.

She knew intuitively that each life was individual and precious, and each path had to be walked alone, step-by-step along the road to initiation. Eventually, greater knowledge and understanding would reveal the true beauty of who they were. And the light grew brighter and brighter and the spirit and angelic hosts irradiated all that was before them. The intensity and the brightness spread out wider and wider until not a margin of darkness remained.

Then the angelic hosts sang with a purity of tone, which

was crystal clear as a bell. Higher and higher in pitch than anything Emma had heard before. She knew that these tones were higher than the ear could pick up. Emma recognised that the Glorias and Hosannas ringing out into the world, would normally go unheard. And the music, unlike anything she had heard before had a piquancy, and delicacy all of its own and the tears came to her eyes as she listened to the sound.

And a shaft of light brighter than the surrounding radiance channelled down on to the central stone of the circle. The centre where the highest level of energy seemed to localise.

She knew about earth energy points, which the ancients were in contact with. Just as man had energy points in his body so the earth had these energy points, connecting different parts of the world.

And she saw Scan move across to that centre of light and place the beautiful bowl with the yellow jewel in the gap in the central stone. And she watched the fluctuation in colour and depth as it caught the light. And Emma saw minor channels of light directed outward to each individual, highlighting the learnt colours of experience. All different, but blending together to make a pattern of colour of indescribable beauty, mingling and mixing with a continual movement of light and colour.

The elves and the goblins, the fairies and the divas and the angelic hosts, the wild animals and the domesticated sat alongside each other in peace.

Everywhere the intensified colour of flowers of the most soft delicate hues and tones unlike anything she had seen before, as though an artist's palette had come to life with a new vibrancy and delicacy.

It was so beautiful that Emma felt her heart move, and that outgoing flow of love ran down her arms and out into the world.

This was a new experience and she knew instinctively

that everyone was being helped to be part of what was happening. They were being bathed in that healing light and being changed, made whole, made clear of all disease.

The peace and serenity cascaded like a waterfall of golden light over all, over everything.

Emma held her breath in awe and wonder as the colours flowed and spilled over everything. And the gold of the amber stone was growing in intensity, becoming brighter and brighter.

Emma looked up in the sky and the two moons were moving closer and closer together until they were superimposed one upon the other and the light flooded down on to the amber stone in the centre of the circle, all its energy activating the force it held within it, and it glowed with a yellow heat and a fire which sent arrows of light far out into the distance.

Emma could not believe the beauty of what surrounded her, because even though she was at a distance she was part of what was happening as surely as if she had been there.

And her heart sang. The universe was singing. Everything near and far was part of that song of praise, of harmony. The elementals were swinging around in rings. The elves, the imps, each in individual rings, dancing and singing, joining in this universal song, this psalm of rejoicing. Then the fairies with their delicate, iridescent hues.

Emma could never again disbelieve in the existence of life forms other than her own. And above, spirits on different levels of development. Each within the other. Emma knew intuitively that the higher her vision went, the brighter the light was and the closer was this area to the total God force. She knew that angels were just spirit beings of great light. And each and all were part of that light. And the world was flooded with beauty and the iridescent rainbow delicacy penetrated everything substantial, yet was insubstantial and ephemeral.

And the light from the stone was everywhere. There were no nooks and crannies that it did not penetrate and influence.

She remembered that it had been foretold by the astrologers that when the line up of the planets was right that some big change would occur in the world. Was this the change that the ancients had said would happen?

And the individual circles broke up and all intermingled with great love and peace and harmony. Then the light grew less bright, gently the vision withdrew, faded and became insubstantial as a rainbow disappearing from sight. Then all was gone. Only the memory remained and a golden glow in the sky.

Emma saw people picking themselves up. Thanbodians struggling to an upright position and gazing around in a stunned way at the Plain of Sol. She knew a great victory had been won. A greater understanding had broken into the density of the land and its people. Part of that peace was within her.

She knew that all would be well and in her heart wondered why she had been chosen to be part of that change and her heart sang with joy at the participation, as each individual turned one to the other in greeting, and embraced one the other, and looked long and hard into each other's face.

They seemed to read there that war between country and individual would be of the past. They would be accepted for what they were and not forced to conform, but allowed to be. Each person walking his own path to inner freedom. The radiancy of that knowledge shone in their faces and seemed to make their physical selves lighter and brighter and more purposeful.

Emma stood and marvelled at what had happened. Then her consciousness seemed to shift and what was before her changed and faded out of existence. She heard the voice of her mother saying, "Time to get up. It's a beautiful morning, you're wasting the first day of the holidays lying in bed."

She looked at the flower print on the curtains and the teddy bear with the pile worn bare and the pictures of pop stars on the wall and all the other things, which she had collected over the years and wondered if it had all been a dream.

She lay there quietly in the stillness of the room and pondered with wonder at the remembrance, and she felt as though the reality of it was still with her. Then she pulled herself out of bed and stretched and something fell to the floor and it emitted a silver, scintillating tone which rang out loud and clear into the early morning light and drew the birds to her window sill where they sang with a vibrancy of the early days of Spring and she was filled with joy and happiness.